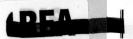

I've been living a double life. Oh sure, on the surface, I might seem low-key. The people who've seen my office—and weren't too traumatized to speak afterward—would say I lean more toward chaos theory than perfectionism. But they just don't know the sleep I've lost agonizing over the best way to phrase a single sentence. Or about that one Thanksgiving when, admittedly, I became a tad uptight in my attempts to mash the perfect potatoes. Hey, there is such a thing as smoothing out *too many* lumps.

I've learned the hard way that there's a fine line between trying your best and trying too hard. But Jocelyn McBride, my alter-ego heroine, was raised to be a perfectionist and is convinced that she can solve all her problems by giving one hundred and ten percent—even when Joss's newest problem is her ex-lover Hugh Brannon. When Joss and Hugh are made co-workers through an unexpected business merger, her well-choreographed life spins out of control like a drunken dance troupe. But through it all, she and Hugh learn that the secret to life and love, as with mashed potatoes, is balance.

If you enjoy Joss's story, please check out my Web site at www.tanyamichaels.com for excerpts of upcoming books, reader giveaways and other fun information.

Happy Reading!

Tanya

"Joss, I don't want anything to drink. I want—"

"There's no good way to end that sentence, Hugh," she said softly. "Except possibly 'the Cowboys to get to the Super Bowl this year.' But then, I'd probably be offended that you're thinking about football right now."

"Trust me, I'm not."

Trust him? Easier said than done.

"I've missed you," he told her.

"We work together," Joss reminded him.

"That didn't stop us before."

As arguments went, it wasn't his most convincing. "Yes, and didn't that turn out swimmingly?"

Hugh wisely dropped the issue, choosing to return his dishes to the kitchen, then hovered in the hallway. "I guess I should go?"

As opposed to stay and have delicious sex? "I'd see you out, but..."

"You need to stay off that ankle."

True. But what she'd really been thinking was that her knees might still be too weak from his kisses for her to stand.

Not Quite
As Advertised

Tanya Michaels

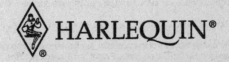

TORONTO • NEW YORK • LONDON
AMSTERDAM • PARIS • SYDNEY • HAMBURG
STOCKHOLM • ATHENS • TOKYO • MILAN • MADRID
PRAGUE • WARSAW • BUDAPEST • AUCKLAND

ISBN 0-373-44202-5

NOT QUITE AS ADVERTISED

Copyright © 2004 by Tanya Michna.

This edition published by arrangement with Harlequin Books S.A.

® and TM are trademarks of the publisher. Trademarks indicated with ® are registered in the United States Patent and Trademark Office, the Canadian Trade Marks Office and in other countries.

www.eHarlequin.com

Printed in U.S.A.

ABOUT THE AUTHOR

RITA® Award-nominated author Tanya Michaels has been reading books all her life, and romances have always been her favorite. She is thrilled to be writing for Harlequin—and even more thrilled that the stories she makes up now qualify as "work" and exempt her from doing the dishes after dinner. The 2001 Maggie Award winner lives in Georgia with her two wonderful children and a loving husband whose displays of support include reminding her to quit writing and eat something. Thankfully, between her husband's thoughtfulness and that stash of chocolate she keeps at her desk, Tanya can continue writing her books in no danger of wasting away.

For more information on Tanya, her upcoming releases and periodic giveaways, please visit her Web site at www.tanyamichaels.com.

Books by Tanya Michaels

HARLEQUIN FLIPSIDE
6—WHO NEEDS DECAF?

HARLEQUIN DUETS
96—THE MAID OF DISHONOR

HARLEQUIN TEMPTATION
968—HERS FOR THE WEEKEND
986—SHEER DECADENCE

With heartfelt thanks to that loopy group of women who've given me unfailing friendship and support, advice on everything from babies to food to grammar, and more laughs than classic *SNL* and *Python* combined. Bless you guys for always being there.

1

JOCELYN MCBRIDE was in hell. Who knew it would look so much like an airport?

In lieu of the more obvious horns and tail, the smug little man at the gate check-in counter was sporting an orange-and-purple vest with the East West Air logo, but, judging by the barely suppressed glee in his expression, he would enjoy the eternal torment of others. "Oh, I'm *so* sorry, ma'am, but the plane has left the gate. Perhaps you were unaware of our company's policy encouraging passengers to check in at least an hour in advance?"

"My flight out of Detroit was delayed," Joss explained breathlessly, still winded from sprinting through O'Hare.

After a dismal breakfast meeting that morning, when she'd been told her agency was not getting the account, then being grounded for an hour because of mechanical difficulties, she'd finally arrived here in Chicago. She'd jogged up to the departure gate just in time to see her plane's backside as it turned on the tarmac. That had been the topper—being mooned by a 717.

Eyebrows raised, the man with the receding hairline and conspicuously absent name badge consulted his computer screen. "This was a connection? I'm not showing any EWA—"

"It was with a different airline." Joss enjoyed her job with Visions Media, a much smaller advertising agency than the last company she'd worked for, but the much smaller expense budget left something to be desired. Convenient travel plans, for instance.

"Oh, I see." He smirked. "You chose to go with one of our competitors. How unfortunate they proved unreliable."

Client-oriented herself, Joss had marveled in the past over the occasional rude waitress, condescending bank teller or postal worker who seemed on the verge of going, well, postal. Today, she should have expected it. The EWA agent was just par for the course here at purgatory's country club.

"I realize the plane's taxied away from the gate, but it hasn't actually left the ground, right?" Hoping to win him over while there was still time, Joss attempted a bright smile. The result felt muddled, like the face-lift her mom's friend Lacey had had. "Is there any chance we could call it back?"

"Oh, sure. We make it a point to inconvenience hundreds of passengers to accommodate the one who couldn't be here at final boarding call." His sarcasm sent her newly risen hopes plummeting like the stock market on Black Thursday.

Fighting the urge to abandon her own people skills and grab Mr. Helpful by his ugly polyester ascot, she reminded herself that any hint of violence would send airport security swarming.

Then again, a flying body tackle by a well-muscled guy would be the most action she'd seen since her breakup last month with David. *And let's face it, David wasn't anything to write home about.* No man had been, not since—

The gate agent heaved an impatient sigh. "There's another flight in a couple of hours. Do you want me to book you on it, or not? According to the schedule, I should've been on my break three and a half minutes ago."

And she should be en route to Dallas! The ADster awards gala was tonight, and her More Than Common Scents campaign for a local aromatherapist had been nominated.

"Yes." She spoke through involuntarily clenched teeth. "Please get me on the very next plane."

Joss had been in the ADster running last year, too, but had placed a frustrating second behind then coworker Hugh Brannon, who'd been nominated for a separate campaign. At the time, she'd been working for the ultraprestigious Mitman Marketing Solutions...and had only recently ended her affair with charming, competitive, sexy-as-sin Hugh. He was an incredible lover, but somehow his stealing a salon account out from under her had quelled her warmer feelings for the man.

Losing a promotion to him prior to the awards had been harsh; taking home a silver certificate in light of his gold trophy had been rock bottom. But, as any good geologist knew, you could get a lot lower than rock—there were whole layers of iron and crust and molten core. Joss probably shouldn't have been so surprised when, a week later, her mother had called to ask if Joss was watching the news. Mitman Marketing had been charged with fraud. So much for prestige.

Now Joss was with Visions Media Group and back on top of her game, more than ready to face Hugh tonight. One of his print campaigns with the full-service agency Kimmerman and Kimmerman was up against her aromatherapy ads. Her employer was overjoyed just to have a nomination, but Joss wanted to win. She hadn't been raised to appreciate second place.

Behind the counter, Mr. Helpful stabbed a few computer keys with his index finger. Then he stole a pointed glance at his watch—clearly her cue to gen-uflect with gratitude for his postponing his break to do her the favor of a seat assignment.

Next time, she was flying the *friendly* skies.

He handed over the new boarding pass in its or-ange-and-purple paper jacket. "I suggest you come to the gate early so that we don't have to do this again."

Deciding a mumbled thanks was the wisest, if not the most satisfying response, she walked away. As she headed for the lounge on the other side of the cor-ridor, she dug her cell phone out of her purse and hit the preprogrammed button for the office.

"Visions Media Group." The male voice that an-swered didn't belong to receptionist Cherie Adams.

"This is Joss… Nick?"

"Yeah." Like numerous advertising groups these days, Visions was small, made up of fewer than a dozen people. But they weren't so tiny that the graphic design/IT guy usually played secretary.

"Where's Cherie?"

"She had a dental emergency," he said. "Where are *you?* Over Indiana?"

"No." She sat on a padded vinyl stool in the passenger bar and darted a malevolent glance over her shoulder toward the now abandoned gate counter. "I missed my connection out of O'Hare."

"Missed your connection? Joss, the awards are tonight!"

You don't say. Nick was a good guy, though, so she spared him her cranky sarcasm.

"I'm on a flight at five," she said. "My car's at DFW, and if traffic's not too bad, I should be able to just make it. I'm going to call Emily now. If she can drop off my dress and shoes, can you meet me in the lobby tonight?"

"Sure... How'd it go with Neely-Richards?"

"The presentation seemed to go well, but then Neely told me over breakfast that they 'went in another direction.'" The industry lingo for "thanks, but not a chance" stuck uncomfortably in her throat. "They voted last night to name a firm in New York their exclusive agency of record."

"To handle promotion of stores they're opening out West? Too bad they didn't come to this brilliant decision before we ate the expense of the trip."

"It happens." She attempted to sound philosophical. Winners did not cultivate bad attitudes. "Don't worry about it. I have two meetings next week I feel really good about."

"Right. Sorry things aren't going better now, though."

So was she. Her boss, Wyatt Allen, had been a bit preoccupied lately, almost tense, and if he was worried about business, this contract would have really helped.

"See you in a few hours, then," Nick said. "It would really *stink* if you didn't get to accept your aromatherapy trophy in person."

She groaned. "There's a reason we hired you to do visual and not copy." Her friend's sense of humor was a lot like the common cold—there was no known cure, and you just had to suffer through it. She liked his optimism, though.

Her second call was to her best friend, business-communications professor Emily Gruber. "Hey, Em. It's me. You have a minute before class?"

"You mean the sixty seconds I'm using to magically finish all the grading I put off?" Emily's sigh was rueful. "I know, I know—I'm worse than the students. But these mock cover letters and résumés make me fear for the future of the country."

Joss laughed. "It's barely October. You have the rest of the semester to whip your students into shape." Well, not so much "whip," as gently nudge. Emily's classes always had high numbers because she was known for being something of a soft touch. "I won't keep you, but can I ask a quick favor?"

"At least you ask," her friend said cheerfully. "Simon just lets me know what I can do for him."

Joss bit back her first instinctive reply. Much as she loved Emily, Joss had never really warmed to Em's boyfriend—Dr. Simon Lowe, Ph.D. and SOB. The pompous man took Emily for granted. But, since Joss herself was calling to impose, perhaps now wasn't the optimal time to lecture her friend on telling people no.

"I'm stuck in Chicago," Joss said, "and have the ADsters tonight. Would it be possible for you to run by my house later, pick up my dress and some essentials and leave them at the office?"

"Sure, no problem. Dulcie will appreciate the extra visit." Since Joss didn't know any of her new neighbors very well, Emily had agreed to stop by and feed the chocolate-point Siamese while Joss was gone. "Will you have time to get to the office, or is someone bringing your clothes to the awards?"

"Nick's taking care of that. You are an absolute lifesaver, Em. The only other person with a key is my mother."

And, at the moment, Joss would rather lie on the runway and let a plane roll over her than call Vivian McBride. No doubt her mom would have had the forethought to travel with her ensemble for the evening, just to be safe. Plus, if Joss phoned, Vivian would automatically ask about the results of the business trip. Nothing solidified the thrill of failing quite like sharing the failure with her mother.

"Just let me know what to grab," Emily said. "We want to make sure you look fabulous for your big win."

As Joss listed everything she needed, she experienced a twinge of anxiety. First, Nick's remark about Joss taking home the trophy, now Emily's assurance of a "big win." Optimism or not, the word *jinx* came to mind.

She was proud of her work—you didn't succeed in advertising by feigning modesty—but underestimating the opposition would be a mistake. Hugh Brannon could charm his way into a nunnery, and he often produced campaigns as slick as he was...even if some of his accounts with Kimmerman and Kimmerman did rely heavily on the marketing equivalent of name-dropping, substituting celebrities for creativity.

"Joss? You still there?"

"Yeah. I was just trying to think if there was anything else I need. Thanks again, I really appreciate this."

"You're welcome. And good luck tonight!"

She needed it, Joss thought as she punched in her home number to check her machine. Two messages, both for Bob—the apparent former owner of her new phone number. She tried not to think about the fact that he got more calls than she did, but her mind just wandered back to her nervousness about tonight.

Hugh Brannon had already beat her once, and even if he didn't pull it off a second time, there were four other deserving nominees in the regional print-campaign category. Her stomach knotted. *Where's your winning attitude, Jocelyn?*

Maybe it had taken the flight to Dallas without her.

Since her plane from Chicago left on schedule and she hadn't checked any luggage for the airline to lose, Joss arrived at the downtown awards site with eight and a half minutes to spare. *And here I thought I'd be pressed for time to get ready.* Despite knowing she didn't have to be inside the ballroom at the exact time printed on her invitation, years of hearing "Perfection begins with punctuality, Jocelyn" rang in her head.

Ask not for whom the annoying voice tolls...

As promised, Nick Sheperd stood in the hotel lobby, shifting his weight and looking uncomfortable.

"Thanks so much," she greeted him breathlessly. "I couldn't very well wear this to the awards." "This" was a utilitarian navy pantsuit perfect for business travel, over a crisp white blouse that had been rendered considerably less so when a fellow passenger dumped his soft drink on her midturbulence.

"I'm just glad you're finally here," Nick said, a relieved expression on his lean, unshaven face. "I was beginning to feel stupid standing with a dress and a bunch of flowers."

"Flowers?" She'd noticed her garment bag draped over a nearby powder-blue love seat. Taking a second look, she saw the vase of red roses on the tiled floor, and sighed. "David, I presume?"

It was identical to the arrangement she'd received from her ex-boyfriend on Valentine's Day, her birthday and their six-month anniversary. They hadn't made it to seven.

Nick nodded, the overhead light reflecting off the mousse he'd used to carefully spike his hair tonight. "He sent them to the office, and I brought them with me so they wouldn't wilt over the weekend."

She studied the flowers. *When you care enough to send the very cliché.* Maybe she should be touched that David remembered her big night, but it was hard to work up any real emotion now when he hadn't shown any throughout their relationship. While she'd given the relationship her customary one hundred and ten percent, David fell back on pat gestures.

He was the type of person who preferred the ease of gift certificates to actually picking out something personal and would buy ten copies of the same generic birthday card to send to friends and family. She, on the other hand, had already started looking for the perfect Christmas present for Emily, even though it was only October. Joss was in the habit of finishing her holiday shopping before Thanksgiving.

In all fairness to David, he'd never made an effort to hide his minimalist approach to relationships. One of the things she'd found attractive about him in the beginning was how different he'd been from charming ubersalesman Hugh, who gave women the same full-court press he gave prospective clients. Joss should have ended things with David sooner, but breakups were failures, and she'd been loath to admit another romantic defeat.

She scooped up her garment bag, needing to correct her soda-stained clothes and limp travel hair before anyone else saw her. "I'm going to dash into the ladies' room and change. See you inside?"

"Or…I could wait here if you want. Then I can run your stuff out to your car while you go in and mingle with more important people." His hazel eyes twinkled. "I know it'll cause you actual physical pain if you're late."

Ignoring the teasing dig, she smiled. "That would be great, Nick. I'd love a chance to talk to Wyatt before the dinner presentation starts." She was hoping she could pick up some clues in casual conversation about what was bothering her employer.

Perhaps she was overreacting to his recently quiet mood and a few frowns, but a little paranoia was understandable after her last employer had been indicted for fraud.

Carrying her dress and purse, Joss hurried toward the bathroom. She hung the garment bag on the inside of a stall door, then quickly stripped. As she wiggled into a pair of panty hose, the nylons snagged on her thumbnail, and the resulting run spread like a jagged fungus of tiny multiplying rectangles. Giving in to a rare impulse, she let loose a satisfying string of obscenities that summed up her day thus far.

"*Ahem*," someone said from an adjoining stall.

Whoops.

"Sorry!" Joss called. "Didn't realize anyone else was in here." With the way her day was going, the person she'd offended was tonight's awards presenter. Joss had a brief, painful picture of going up on stage in shredded hose to accept an award from a woman glaring at her.

Joss glanced hopefully at the bottom of the bag. Nestled beneath the hem of her strapless muted red dress, with her shoes and travel jewelry case, was the wished-for extra pair. *Bless you, Em.* The slit in her calf-length skirt was meant to reveal a little leg, and Joss would have worried all night that the run was visible.

One shimmy, zip and shrugged-into bolero jacket later, she was fully dressed. She hung her discarded suit in the garment bag and opened the door, glancing sheepishly at the pinch-faced woman washing her hands.

What Joss would've liked was time to completely redo her makeup and put curlers in her shoulder-length layered blond hair. What she settled for was a loose chignon and fresh lipstick. She exchanged her small gold hoop earrings for a pair of elongated ruby teardrops, then returned to the lobby, where she found Nick pacing and jostling his car keys.

He stopped long enough to grin in approval. "You did that in five minutes? If you ever decide to have a meaningless affair with a much younger guy, let me know."

Four years was not *much* younger. "I can't think about you that way, Nicky. You're like the annoying little brother I never had."

He laughed and held out his hand for her stuff. "Keys? Wyatt and Penelope just went inside."

Wyatt Allen, a grizzled veteran of the advertising world, ran Visions Media Group. His wife, Penelope, had made participating in various charities her full-time occupation, but she chipped in from time to time at Visions, helping with paperwork and receptionist duties.

Joss handed Nick her key ring, and he pivoted to go, pausing at the last second with an expression of endearing uncertainty shadowing his face. "How do *I* look?"

She smiled inwardly. Ad execs stuck to a professional dress code, but people who were strictly on the creative end were allowed, even encouraged, to project a less orthodox image. Everyone at Visions knew Nick aspired to a wardrobe that would help keep Ralph Lauren in business, but in an underdressed attempt to look the part, he now wore an iridescent unstructured blazer with a striped shirt and dark funky jeans.

"Like the opening act at a rock concert," she told him.

"Thanks." Nick turned toward the revolving doors. "I think."

Joss went to the ballroom, pausing just inside the doorway to let her eyes adjust to the dimmed chandeliers and flickering candles on the white linen tablecloths. Bland jazz played through speakers in the back of the room, but it was mostly drowned out by the hum of conversation. Maybe being late was no longer fashionable—the impressive crush of people made it difficult to find the round table reserved for Visions Media Group.

"Quite a crowd tonight," a man said near her ear.

She almost jumped. Taking a deep breath, she steeled herself against Hugh Brannon's husky bedroom voice and the bubbles of nervous anticipation fizzing through her system. Obviously the crowd wasn't big *enough*.

2

"Hugh." Joss turned, confident in her composed expression. She'd won plenty of poker games, this one was just played without cards. "It's a pleasure to see you."

Viscerally speaking, her words were true. What woman *wouldn't* be pleased to see a tall tuxedoed man who looked like Hugh? With his thick black hair, short in the back but longer and sexily disheveled around his face, his laser-blue eyes and finely chiseled flawless features, he was hot without even trying. But then he'd smile.

Hugh Brannon's teasing grin and accompanying dimples could convince female Eskimos to line up to buy ice.

"A pleasure?" he echoed. "My, how we in marketing do bend the truth."

"Speak for yourself." Joss smiled sweetly. "*My* ads use honesty and ingenuity."

"And mine use...?"

"Overpaid celebrities, mostly."

"Well, I do work for a large agency with the budget for network commercials and well-known stars." His tone was annoyingly indulgent. "I guess you're in a different position."

The streamlined Visions Media Group might not produce glamorous spots for national television, but some of advertising's most memorable campaigns, such as the milk mustache, had been print. And for all that Hugh liked to needle her, he oversaw his share of regional work. To hear him tell it, you'd think he was single-handedly responsible for the ads played during the Super Bowl.

She scoffed. "You're not up against me because of national commercials."

He swept his gaze over her. "I miss being up against you."

His words caught her off guard, and a pang of desire tightened her midsection. Should she glare, which he fully deserved, or look away in case she blushed tellingly? Not an oh-I'm-embarrassed-by-your-sexual-references girlish blush. An oooh-that-sounds-good-to-me-too flush of color. She might have a great bluffing expression, but there wasn't much she could do about her fair skin.

"So…" Hugh glanced around. "Donald's not with you tonight?"

She didn't bother correcting him since he knew perfectly well her ex-boyfriend's name was David. There had been an uncomfortable encounter at a convention in Houston over the summer, and Hugh had childishly insisted on calling David "Dale" all night.

"We're not seeing each other anymore," she said.

He shook his head. "Broke his heart, too, huh?"

Please. As if *she* were the one who'd hurt *him*? "At least he had one."

Instead of arguing, he brought out the big guns—

the seductive smile that lit his eyes and managed to be both boyish and enticingly adult. "You look fantastic, Joss."

So did he. "I certainly think so."

He chuckled at her cool response, and the low, rich laugh turned her insides to traitorous goo.

"What about you, no date tonight?" Ordinarily, she wouldn't have shown the slightest interest in his love life, but she was willing to make an exception since he'd broached the topic.

"Of course not." He feigned shock. "What woman could compare to you?"

Infuriating man. Which, come to think of it, was redundant.

"I forgot how full of it you are," she said.

"Really?" His smile vanished, and he brushed a finger across her cheek. "I haven't been able to forget a thing about you."

It was a pitch, she reminded herself, a sale. Hugh was an ad man who went with what he thought the target audience wanted to hear. She should end this exchange, but she didn't want to be the one to walk away. If only Nick would come in, she could excuse herself gracefully.

Since it didn't look as if anyone was bringing her a file in a cake, she'd have to spring her own escape. "We shouldn't stand in the doorway like this."

"True. Buy you a drink?"

"Very generous…considering it's an open bar."

"It sounded more gallant than, wanna go get a free watered-down cocktail with me?"

"Since when do you care about being gallant?" The old pain was numbed but still there, like emotional scar tissue. "I had you pegged more as opportunistic."

His jaw clenched, but then he shrugged. "Have it your way. I just thought maybe you could use a drink before you take second to my first. Again."

Not if there was any justice in the world.

Her nomination this year was a first for Visions Media Group, and though Wyatt was ecstatic about the added credibility it lent his small company, she wouldn't be satisfied with anything less than victory. Somewhere deep down, she questioned how healthy her desire to win was, but her mom had taught her that "also-ran" meant nothing. Besides, knocking Hugh down a peg would be a favor to the universe, benefiting all mankind.

Womankind, at the very least.

And it's not like I've taken ambition to an unwholesome level. She wasn't some unscrupulous nut who'd smear her opponent's reputation, or bribe judges or throw virgin sacrifices into volcanoes to appease deities. Good thing, since the Dallas-Fort Worth area was as lacking in volcanoes as her social circle was in virgins.

Inching away, she went with a more direct brush-off this time. "You'll have to excuse me, Hugh. I see my boss over there, and he wanted a preview of my acceptance speech."

"By all means." He didn't reiterate his prediction of winning, but his smirk conveyed the message all the same.

She ground her back teeth together as she walked away. *Tuxedo, eight hundred and fifteen dollars. Cost of admission to ADster Awards Dinner, ninety dollars. Hugh Brannon's ego, limitless.*

"AND THE GOLD ADSTER goes to…" Tessa St. Martin, a curvy woman in a short sequined dress, opened the envelope.

Hugh waited along with everyone else for the winner's name.

"Kimmerman and Kimmerman's Life in Motion campaign for ATC Tires! Hugh Brannon, account supervisor."

He shoots, he scores.

The crowd didn't exactly go wild, but all around the table, Hugh's co-workers began congratulating him. Individual awards were given out for specific creative contribution, but recognition for an overall campaign went to the person who'd coordinated the client's branding with the agency's work. In this case, Hugh. His friend Mike Denton slapped him on the arm, and Kimmerman Sr. himself reached across the table to shake Hugh's hand.

Standing, Hugh nodded his thanks, but his mind drifted for a second to a fellow nominee across the room. He knew without seeing her that Jocelyn would be smiling graciously—as if she were actually happy for him—and clapping along with everyone else. He also knew she was crushed by her perceived "failure."

She's got to learn not to take these things so seriously, he thought as he walked to the onstage podium.

A competitive man himself, he didn't mean to be hypocritical about Joss's drive. He loved to win, and he was glad for the accolades. It wasn't easy to make all-terrain tires memorable and entertaining, and he'd worked hard to integrate his team's ideas with the client's needs. But Joss worked hard at *everything*. If she kept up her pace and intensity, she'd have an ulcer.

Or worse.

His smile faltered at the dark thought, but he reclaimed it as he took his trophy and kissed Tessa's cheek. Reciting his speech, he checked his impulse to look for Joss. Seeing her earlier tonight had been as galvanizing as the bell ringing at the opening of a boxing match, except fighting wasn't what he wanted to do with her.

Not the only thing, anyway. There'd been a time when their verbal sparring had been a prelude to mind-blowing sex.

Despite telling himself he wouldn't seek Joss out, he continued to subconsciously scan the crowd as he acknowledged the creative team he'd supervised. Ah—there she was, as gorgeous as ever and forcing herself to smile. Looking at her genial expression, no one would ever guess her fondest wish was to see Hugh shish-kebabbed on an open flame.

Last year, she'd shocked him by walking over from Mitman's second reserved table to congratulate him. It had been the only time she'd voluntarily spoken to him between his landing the Stefan's Salons account and their parting of ways during the investigation of Mitman.

He and Joss had worked in client recruitment, in no way associated with the departments accused of selling falsely manufactured data and using exaggerated focus-group numbers to cut costs and research time. But in spite of her blamelessness, after the industry scandal broke, Joss had become even

more determined to prove herself than before—
which he hadn't realized was possible.

Knowing there were other awards still to be presented, Hugh wrapped up his remarks. "There are
doubtless others I could thank, but you all don't want
to listen to me drone on when there are more important people in the room." He winked at Tessa, who
stood stage left.

Tessa was attractive, but she was no Joss McBride.

He returned to his seat, managing not to look in
Joss's direction again, but her features were already
etched on his memory. She was wearing her hair back
tonight, but he preferred it down, softly framing an
oval face with a stubborn chin. Her slim nose and high
forehead added classic elegance, but her smoky jade
eyes and full mouth promised untamed sensuality.

If her face had left an indelible print on his mind,
it was nothing compared to the impression her body
had left on his. Joss could be as cool and tart as iced
lemonade when she wanted to be, but he knew from
the three glorious weeks he'd spent in her bed that
the woman burned like living flame. Unfortunately
for him, her passion also led to grudges, and when
he'd won the account she'd been eyeing—and the resulting promotion—she'd refused to forgive him.

Her uncompromising stance was a prime example
of her taking something personally. He'd been doing
his job! Sure, she'd been interested in the account, but
her pitches hadn't accomplished anything, and rivalry
had always been part of their relationship. He certainly
wouldn't have kicked her out of bed if the situation
had been reversed. He wouldn't have kicked her out
of bed for selling state secrets to foreign governments.

More recently, Kristine Dillinger, a woman from his neighborhood, occasionally shared Hugh's bed. Athletic and easygoing, Kristine was always up for a great weekend, whether it was going to a bed-and-breakfast in the country with early-morning hiking, or pizza and a leisurely night at his place. As long as they were both single, they got together when they felt like it and owed each other no phone calls or explanations in between. Their friendship was as comfortable as it was casual.

No where-did-he-see-himself-in-five-years, what-kind-of-provider-would-he-be analysis. He hated dates that felt like job interviews. Maybe she didn't set off the internal bells and whistles that Joss had, but time spent with Kristine was a helluva lot more relaxing. He would have invited her tonight, but she would have been bored. *He* was bored by now, and he was one of the evening's honorees.

A few months ago, he might've taken tonight more seriously, but he'd learned to loosen up. Unlike some people.

When the awards presentation ended, he found himself trapped in conversation with a gregarious copywriter from WOW Concepts. Hugh nodded at the copywriter's predictions about the Dallas economy, but his focus was really on Joss as she moved through the throng of well-wishers. She'd taken off the scarlet-and-gold jacket she'd worn earlier, and the smooth curves of her exposed shoulders left him wanting to see more. His body hummed with awareness as she drew closer.

And what's another word for that awareness? Tension. Joss was often intense, or tense, period. He didn't need that in his life.

But needing and wanting were different. He knew from firsthand experience that, in the right circumstances, her intense focus was pretty damn hot.

Having abandoned all pretense of being involved in the conversation, Hugh glanced back at the copywriter. "I'm sorry, I just noticed an old friend trying to get my attention. Would you excuse me?"

He freed himself, but hadn't taken two steps in Joss's direction before she reached him.

"Hugh." Her expression, both regal and grimly determined, called to mind heroic martyrs of bygone eras. Joss of Arc. "I just wanted to say congratulations."

"Thanks." He spared her the condescending crap about how, win or lose, it was an honor to be nominated and how her campaign had been deserving, too.

"Well." She shifted her weight. "Guess I'll see you again next year."

The Dallas advertising community wasn't so big that they never ran into each other, but she certainly didn't seek him out. She was only speaking to him now because she felt obligated, the way football rivals shook hands after the game. Over her shoulder, Hugh noticed her boss, Wyatt Allen, shaking hands with Robert Kimmerman Sr. Graciously accepting second place must be in Vision's mission statement.

Having fulfilled her obligation, Joss turned to go, but Hugh found he didn't want to give her up yet. She'd always sparked something inside him, for better or worse, and he'd forgotten just how *alive* he felt around her.

"Wait…I never did buy you that drink." Even as the words left his mouth, he wondered what he was doing. The woman detested him.

So you have nothing to lose. Besides, she might surprise him. Nostalgic interludes between ex-lovers happened all the time, and if she recalled their three weeks together with the same—

She narrowed her eyes in a scowl that brought his happy train of thought to a screeching halt. "You have *got* to be kidding me, Brannon."

"What? A drink's harmless."

"Harmless, my butt." She crossed her arms over her chest. "You're getting that look. Don't even try to deny it."

It had been worth a shot. "I seem to recall your liking 'that look,'" he said with an unrepentant grin.

"I was young and stupid."

"You were twenty-six. You're barely twenty-eight now. And, Jocelyn, you've *never* been stupid."

For a fleeting victorious moment, he had her speechless. But nothing good lasted forever.

"Everyone makes mistakes," she quipped. "You were just an easy way to meet my quota."

"You wound me."

"I try."

Didn't he know it. Whether it was taking Southwestern cooking classes, futile attempts to train her cat or fleecing everyone else at the table in high-stakes poker, she exerted the same level of effort. Why couldn't she have unproductive noncompetitive fun once in awhile?

And what degree of control-freak insanity did it take for someone to try to train a *cat?*

Hugh sighed. It wasn't that he had no work ethic, it was just that his brother Craig's heart attack had been a startling wake-up call. "Take care of yourself, J."

"I... You, too." She regarded him curiously, then shook her head. Within moments, she'd merged into the crowd, a flash of red among less colorful individuals.

As he drove home later, Hugh told himself it was best Joss hadn't taken him up on his offer of a nightcap. Given their history, they would have ended up trying to outdrink one another, and alcohol poisoning was not his idea of a good time. Hugh may have gained new perspective since the collapse of his older brother, the attorney, this summer, but he still had a competitive nature thirty years in the making.

Growing up, he and his two brothers had competed over everything from athletics to academics to attention from their parents. There had been some friction—particularly between Hugh, to whom many things came easily, and Craig, who resented "losing" to someone three years his junior—but most of the brothers' fighting had been of the short-lived let's-just-deck-each-other-then-go-for-beer variety. Overall, the pressure they put on one another had spurred them to higher achievements. Since college, no one had challenged Hugh quite like that.

Until he'd met Joss.

Both ambitious junior execs on the fast-track to success, they'd been natural rivals for each other. Everyone said opposites attracted, but he and Joss mirrored each other, and he'd never wanted a woman more. In some ways, he'd been in peak form when working with her, but his time with Joss had also made him more like his workaholic brother Craig.

Hugh had once thought he and Joss brought out

the best in each other. It was equally possible they brought out the worst.

DESPITE A BRIGHT NOONDAY SUN, the breeze that carried mist from the fountain in Williams Square was enough to chill Joss's skin.

Emily, however, didn't seem to mind. She nudged Joss off the sidewalk, toward the nine bronze mustangs caught in a frozen gallop across the plaza. The fountain sculpture was one of Emily's favorite places, and they walked by anytime they had lunch in Las Colinas. Today, they'd shared stromboli at an Italian café overlooking Mandalay Canal. Joss had filled her friend in on the details of last night, and Emily had told her about the good book she'd read after Simon blew off their date for a "networking opportunity" with one of the college deans.

"Aren't you cold?" Joss demanded. She had on a long-sleeved henley, while her brunette friend wore short sleeves.

"No, why?"

Why, indeed. Joss freely admitted that, of the two of them, Emily was warmer—inside and out. Which was why she deserved someone who fully appreciated her.

"Hey, Em…do you ever think about what it would be like to be with someone besides Simon?"

Emily's eyes widened. "You mean like cheating on him?"

"No, I meant if things didn't work out. Hypothetically."

"Why wouldn't they? Do you think I'm doing something wrong?"

"Of course not! Like I said, it was strictly a hypothetical question. I didn't mean to alarm you." Seeking divine assistance, Joss rolled her eyes heavenward. "Simon's lucky to have you. Don't let him make you feel inferior."

"He's not 'making' me feel anything. You know how I am, Joss." With a sigh, Emily sat on a shadowed ledge near the fountain. "We aren't all born with your self-confidence."

Born with confidence…or just born to a very determined mother?

A memory surfaced of an elementary-school choir recital—Joss had loved to sing, despite tentative pitch, and she'd been looking forward to the concert. But when all the parents had filed into the auditorium, her knees had started knocking in time to the pianist's metronome. Her voice squeaky with nerves, she'd still managed to warble through her stage fright.

She'd been filled with a huge sense of accomplishment and renewed confidence…until her mother announced on the drive home that she wasn't about to let her daughter make such a public fool of herself again. If Jocelyn wanted to sing, Vivian would help her do it well. A week later, Joss had begun private voice lessons, with her mother's full support.

The kind of support that ensured job security for therapists.

Giving up the sun that hadn't been keeping her warm anyway, Joss sat next to her friend in the shade. "Trust me, Em, there are *plenty* of things I'm bad at. And you're selling yourself short. Not everyone can teach. Or write."

"Sure." Emily pitched a penny into the softly gurgling water, and Joss wondered what today's wish had been. "Put me on the other side of a piece of paper, or in front of a whole class, I'm fine. It's one-on-one interactions that make me nervous."

This came as no surprise to Joss. The two women had met when Mitman did some publicity work for the university, and though they'd hit it off pretty quickly, Emily was shy. The middle child between two boisterous brothers, Em was known for being quiet and accommodating—qualities that had led to her being hurt more than once, but also made her a soothing person to be around. Joss, at the other end of the spectrum, knew she wasn't exactly low-key, and appreciated the balance her friend helped provide. When Joss had first met David, she'd hoped he might be the romantic equivalent of a male Emily.

He'd been more the romantic equivalent of a brick.

What business did she really have trying to push Em to the realization that Simon was all wrong for her? Joss hadn't had any more lasting success in her love life than her friend, whose pre-Simon relationships had included a compulsive liar and a man who waffled weekly between Em and his ex-wife, but was at least honest about it.

Thankfully, Emily changed the subject away from men entirely. "I was impressed with the improvements on the house, by the way. I went over to feed Dulcie, expecting a certified disaster, but it wasn't as bad as you made it sound. I think maybe you're just expecting too much too soon."

"Who, me?"

The new house—rather, the seventy-year-old house she'd recently purchased—was either her pride and joy, or the albatross mortgaged around her neck for the next three decades. Depending on what day you asked.

She'd been en route to a subdivision of shinier modern homes with programmable digital thermostats and updated appliances when she'd driven by the neglected two-story for sale. It hadn't been what she was looking for, but it *had* stood out among the houses she'd seen, with their cookie-cutter floor plans and treeless postage-stamp-size yards. Ultimately, the urge to perfect had been irresistible—she could buy the house at a bargain and reshape its raw appeal into her dream home.

Of course, recent business demands had thus far impeded her brilliant renovation schemes. And the "bargain" was costing her a fortune.

Emily's continued reassurance was cheering. "The refinished dining-room floor looks terrific—I don't understand why anyone carpeted over that hardwood in the first place!"

"Thanks. I plan to put hardwood in the foyer, too." It was on her ever-growing to-do list.

"And I was really impressed with the progress on the wraparound porch. I made it all the way to the door without once worrying I was going to crash through rotting steps."

Progress *was* being made, but the porch would have been done by now if the man Joss had hired didn't have all manner of excuses for delaying. Weather, supplies, an emergency across town, his astrologist telling him Jupiter was in the wrong house for him to handle nails that day... Patience, she reminded herself. Rome wasn't build in a day.

Maybe Caesar couldn't find a decent contractor, either.

"All right, I suppose I am a little impatient. I just can't wait to see what everything will look like once it all comes together." Whatever century *that* was. "I've got to get a new water heater, though. And I still haven't decided on colors for the downstairs bathroom or my bedroom."

Emily laughed. "I would've decorated the bedroom first and let everything else sit for months."

"I don't think 'sitting' is an option for the water heater. It's a disaster waiting to happen, and I haven't finished my room because I just haven't seen anything truly perfect yet. And then there's that hideous kitchen..."

Joss was in the middle of painstakingly stripping the current wallpaper. Current only in the sense that it happened to be on the wall, not that it bore any resemblance to something presently fashionable. She'd been pleased with how easy it was to peel off the busy vertigo-inducing pattern, but then discovered the reason she'd been able to remove the paper so quickly was because it hadn't actually been attached to the wall. Instead, there was a second print—less busy, just as ugly—beneath.

She'd now uncovered three strata left by previous generations. *My kitchen, the suburban archeological dig.* Joss was investigating interesting sociological issues, such as how the hell had avocado and gold become so popular in the first place?

Mercifully, the third layer of paper, a lovely shade

of bordello red, appeared to be the last. Joss didn't expect any more prints to pop up like never-ending clowns out of one of those little circus cars. The bad news, however, was that older wallpapers were considerably more difficult to remove than what was being manufactured these days, especially if the paper turned out to be "nonporous," as her call-girl crimson was.

Now that Joss was back in town after her unsuccessful meeting with Neely-Richards, she needed to buy a puncturing roller and rent a wallpaper steamer. Probably not today, though. She already had a list of errands that might well take her into middle age, including Dulcie's annual vaccinations this afternoon. The fact that the veterinarian was a great-looking guy helped compensate for the Siamese's weeklong grudges after clinic visits. Joss glanced at her watch with a sigh.

"Lunch was great," she said, "but I'm afraid I need to run. I've got to take Dulcie to see the cute vet at three, and I should get around to looking at tile samples for that downstairs bathroom. You don't, by any chance, want to come with me and help narrow down a color scheme, do you?"

"Actually, I have to get going, too." Emily stood. "I've got some work to do before Simon picks me up. We're having an early dinner and catching a movie at that art house he likes."

"*He* likes?"

"I like it, too." Emily's mumbled response didn't change the fact that she went to most of the movies on her "must-see" list with Joss, then reportedly spent her dates with Simon squinting at foreign-film subtitles. "And he's right about me—my horizons could use some broadening."

All right, that did it! There was nothing wrong with Emily. Or her horizons. If Simon couldn't appreciate her, Joss just might have to help her find someone who would.

Hmm, come to think of it, Dan Morris, the cute vet, was single. Joss would have dated him herself, but Dan was a dog person. She was allergic.

"Joss?"

"Uh-huh?"

"Should I be worried?" Emily asked as they turned toward the sidewalk that would lead them back to their respective cars. "For a second there, you had that same look of psychotic determination as when you peeled off the second layer of wallpaper and we found the third. Everything okay?"

Joss smiled, thinking what adorable kids Em and Dr. Dan could have. "Absolutely perfect."

3

AFTER DISCOVERING Dr. Dan had recently started seeing someone and then spending a fruitless hour studying color samples, Joss arrived home Saturday evening with a taupe-tan-rosy-beige migraine and a hissing Siamese who harbored plans to lacerate her while she slept.

Despite the imminent kitty threat, she retired to bed early after a salad and a TV movie. It had been an exhausting week, and she needed rest before she tackled any of the formidable redecorating. She snuggled under the duvet and crashed hard, waking Sunday to a feeling of invigorated well-being...that lasted three and a half seconds.

Then she winced in uncomfortable realization. Damn, she thought as she reached in her nightstand drawer for the plastic aspirin bottle, it was that time of the month.

Brunch with her mother.

Amazing how quickly headache threatened at the thought of seeing Vivian. Joss was tempted to cancel, saying she was under the weather, but mothers didn't fall for that sort of thing—a lesson she'd learned when she'd claimed appendicitis in a fifth-grade attempt to gain more study time for a math test. Of course, she might've been more convincing if she'd been clutching her *right* side.

She stomped toward the shower, wondering what kind of mood the schizophrenic water heater would be in today, and ignored Dulcie's feline smirk from the foot of the bed. The vengeful Siamese, a Christmas present from Vivian three years ago, obviously sensed that Joss's day would be an experience comparable to yesterday's shots. Though Joss and her mother lived in the same urban area, they only saw each other on the first Sunday of each month, meeting for strained brunches. Maybe it was an odd tradition, considering their busy schedules and the lack of effusive affection between them, but they were each all the family the other had.

Today was likely to be even less pleasant than usual, Joss thought as she washed her hair. Vivian had made her mark in the city as a high-end real estate agent, and she hadn't been amused when her only daughter bought a house without once picking up the phone to consult her. *You'd think she would applaud my self-sufficiency.* After all, it was Vivian who had always endorsed striving for excellence and relying only on yourself. Viv's motto was an adjusted version of the army's—Be All You Can Be…because you can't depend on anyone else. A cynical creed, perhaps, but one that had helped her raise a child by herself, while not only holding a job, but becoming something of a local expert in her field. Vivian never accepted anything short of excellence.

Still, Joss thought as she went to her closet and debated what to wear, just once, it might be nice if she and her mother went somewhere casual, where they could relax and catch up and…wait, she must be thinking of someone else's mom. Normally, their monthly brunches were held at a French bistro near Vivian's condominium, but there had recently been a change in chefs. Joss's mother refused to set foot in the place until "culinary integrity" was restored.

Instead, Vivian had picked out the Well-Fed Waif, a place downtown that consistently garnered rave reviews. Joss could attest to the excellent service and food, but these days, she rarely visited the restaurant where she'd once been a regular. Located around the corner from where the Mitman offices had been, the Waif had been a favorite of hers and Hugh's.

It would be heavenly to enjoy the restaurant's eggs Florentine again, she thought as she pulled on a lightweight turtleneck. Of course, since it *had* been a place she and Hugh had visited often and since she'd seen him so recently, he was bound to cross her mind. But that just made today the perfect opportunity for an emotional exorcism. What better way to drive out lingering memories of intimate working dinners and shared glances over morning mimosas than a few hours with her mother?

"If I've done something to offend you," Joss muttered, "just turn me into a dung beetle and get it over with."

Vivian paused in her small talk with the Versace-clad hostess standing behind a stained-wood podium. "Who *are* you talking to, Jocelyn?"

The universe. "Nobody."

"Mumbling isn't very well-bred," her mother reprimanded.

Neither was the four-letter word that had sprung

to Joss's mind when she'd entered the Well-Fed Waif and spotted Hugh Brannon. He sat at a corner table near the decorative fireplace, across from a gentleman who looked about Vivian's age. Obviously the cosmos was having a little joke at Joss's expense.

Hugh. He's everywhere you don't want him to be.

At least he wasn't with a woman. Joss was over him, but that didn't mean she was in a hurry to find him wooing a date at their old table.

Vivian took in the conservative art, the strains of violin overhead and the fresh-cut flowers hanging in glass wall vases, then allowed a small smile of approval. "This place is acceptable."

Geez, Mom, contain your exuberance—what will people say?

Truer to form, Vivian frowned suddenly. "I'm not pleased with the wait, though. If I'm to lunch with clients here, I need to know we'll be seated a bit quicker. You don't waste the time of Important People."

The hostess looked down, busying herself with straightening the reservation book and a basket of mints, clearly abashed, even though Joss and her mother had arrived mere minutes ago.

Vivian had that effect—making people feel their best was inadequate. She would've had da Vinci stammering that of *course* the *Mona Lisa* needed a wider smile, and he didn't know what he'd been thinking! In real estate, Vivian was such a whiz at finding fault with property that by the time her client made an offer—well below asking price—the grateful seller was ready to agree to anything just to offload the dump.

Joss watched as her mother glanced around the

restaurant again, not evaluating the setting itself this time, but looking to see if she knew anyone and whether there were any noteworthy individuals present. "Noteworthy" to Vivian wasn't just someone with enough money to potentially buy or sell in her specialized area of town—although that helped—but anyone with status in the community. Financial security and respectability were what a twenty-year-old and pregnant Vivian had been denied when she'd shared the news of her pregnancy with her fiancé. He'd backed out of the wedding, which was only weeks away, and the appalled McBrides had threatened to disown their daughter if she didn't put the baby up for adoption, convinced single parenthood would ruin the life they'd envisioned for her.

Vivian had vowed to raise the perfect daughter all by herself, refusing her parents' help when they softened a couple of years later. Instead, she'd busted her butt to make money, and as far back as Joss could remember, her mother had taken every opportunity to rub elbows with those who had local prestige—business owners, philanthropists, the deputy mayor. Even now, Joss caught occasional glimpses of what a younger Vivian must have been like, facing abandonment with the determination to prove she was Someone.

"Jocelyn! Do you know who that is over there?"

Nine times out of ten, the answer to this question was no, but Joss dutifully followed her mother's gaze, anyway. *You have got to be kidding me!* For a horrible second, she thought her mom meant Hugh, which would be bad because Vivian wouldn't like finding out her daughter had been involved with a man for almost a month and hadn't mentioned him; much less introduced him. Then Joss realized Vivian meant Hugh's companion, which, come to think of it, was just as bad if it meant Vivian wanted to say hello.

"That's Stanley *Patone*," Vivian said, emphasizing Patone as if the single word should draw the same social recognition as DeNiro, Madonna or Brad and Jen. Then came the dreaded words, "We simply must go over and say hello!"

Life as a dung beetle was looking better all the time.

Reminding herself that she'd survived plenty of encounters with Hugh Brannon and that this would be brief, Joss held her head high and followed her purposeful mother.

Hugh saw them first, doing an astonished double take. Dallas was big enough that they seldom bumped into each other without expecting it beforehand, and he had to be wondering about the petite woman who was so obviously Jocelyn's mother barreling, in her own graceful way, toward him. Joss had always found it oddly poetic that she looked exactly like a younger version of Vivian, with no visible genetic trace of the father she'd never met or the grandparents who had balked at her existence.

"Joss!" Recovering quickly, Hugh rose from his chair. Joss could have sworn jeans were against the Waif's dress code, but he looked so good in them, who would complain? "What a pleasant surprise."

"You two know each other?" Vivian shot a questioning glance over her shoulder, clearly displeased that Joss hadn't armed her with all pertinent data.

"I had the privilege of working with her sister at Mitman," Hugh answered, flashing one of his patented charming grins at Joss's mom. "She didn't tell me she had a sister."

As the smiling and portly Stanley Patone—whoever he was—got to his feet, Vivian shook her head. "Young man, do I look like someone who's easily won over with glib flattery?"

Easily won over? Vivian McBride? *Ha.* Suddenly Joss regretted never having brought Hugh to a Sunday brunch. It would be fun to see him squirm.

Unfortunately, being Hugh, he didn't.

Instead, he grinned. "No, ma'am, but it was worth a shot. If you're anything like your daughter, I need all the help I can get."

Vivian actually chuckled before turning to Stanley, taking his hand in hers. "It's so nice to see you again. Perhaps you don't remember, but we met briefly—"

"At the Fosters' garden party in June," the man finished for her. With his self-conscious expression and a bulky-knit sweater that exaggerated, rather than flattered, his girth, Stanley Patone was less polished and more endearing than Viv's usual Important People. "How could I forget? The mosquitoes were *Jurassic*-size, but you were enchanting."

"Aren't you a dear! Allow me to introduce my daughter, Jocelyn McBride." As Joss shook Stanley's hand, Vivian added, "This is Stanley Patone. Of Patone Power Tools."

Any chance they made wallpaper steamers? Joss nodded obligingly. "Of course. Nice to meet you."

Stanley sighed. "You've never heard of us, have

you? No, it's okay. Too few people have, but Hugh here tells me he can change all that."

Next to her, she noticed Hugh fidget. Clearly, Stanley was teetering on the brink of an ad man's worst nightmare—the prospective client letting another agency know he was looking.

Regaining his composure, Hugh smiled smoothly. "It's practically criminal to be sitting in here on such a gorgeous Sunday morning talking business, I know, but I'm afraid that's what we're doing. We're grateful you lovely ladies stopped by and broke up the monotony, though."

Translation: You should be going now, but really, you wouldn't want to stay anyway because our conversation is dreadfully boring. The man didn't know who he was dealing with.

With a wide isn't-this-a-small-world smile, Vivian placed her hand on Stanley's arm. "You know, Jocelyn's in advertising, as well. She's building that up-and-coming Visions Media Group."

Joss winced inwardly at her mother's version of the truth, which ignored the fact Wyatt Allen had been steadily growing his respected company long before Joss arrived, needing a job after the Mitman fiasco. She did her part, certainly, but she couldn't take single-handed credit for the success Wyatt had been seeding for years.

Stanley gestured toward the two empty chairs. "We've neglected our manners. You will join us, won't you?"

"Absolutely!" Vivian stepped around the power-tool purveyor to squeeze into the far chair against the wall. "It would be our pleasure."

Joss fully expected Hugh to fume over this turn of events, but when she glanced his direction, he looked almost amused.

"Allow me." He pulled her chair out, which would have worked better if she hadn't been trapped *between* Hugh and the chair. "You smell great. Dior?"

She nodded.

"I always loved that perfume on you," he murmured as he helped seat her. "You remember the night—"

"So what's good here?" Joss asked heartily. She remembered many nights. And wanted to discuss none of them.

Vivian stared across the table as though her daughter had grown another head—one with last year's haircut. "Jocelyn, I thought you said you'd been here. Often."

"Y-yes. But not in a long time. Maybe the menu's changed?" Avoiding Hugh's gaze and what was sure to be a smirk, Joss edged her chair closer to Stanley's side of the table.

A discreet beeping came from inside Vivian's handbag—none of this belting out Beethoven's Fifth for her, thank you very much—and she smiled in apology. "I know it's horrid of me to keep the cell on during a meal, but one of my properties is in a bidding war, and the buyers have until six o'clock this evening to outdo each other. Jocelyn, just order for me, won't you?"

Great. Because she so needed the added pressure of potentially screwing that up. But by the time water glasses had been shuffled and the waitress had come by to add the newcomers to the ticket, Joss had regained her composure. As long as she focused on Stanley, she'd be fine. She listened intently while he filled her in on his company.

"We were the 'house brand' for Tucker Home and Hardware for ten years, and turned an extremely lucrative profit," Stanley explained. *Extremely lucrative* certainly clarified her mother's interest in the man. "But Tucker's management didn't fare as well, so when the chain folded, Patone became its own line. We're free to sell everywhere now, but that won't do us any good if no one knows who we are. We don't have nearly the name recognition of, say, Black & Decker."

Joss nodded. "So you're looking for marketing solutions?"

"And solutions he will have," Hugh promised. "I've been brainstorming with some of the best minds in our creative team all week." He might not look actively furious about her intrusion, but he was definitely sending out a back-away-from-the-client vibe. "With any luck, this time next year, I'll be taking home an ADster for the work that brought Patone to the forefront of consumer consciousness."

Joss's jaw clenched at the dig. She hadn't crashed Hugh's brunch with the intention of preying on his client—not that she had enough information on Stanley to bid for his business yet, anyway—but she didn't have to help Hugh win the account for himself, either. "Mr. Patone—"

"Stanley, please."

"I just had an interesting thought. What about a female ad executive? If you go with Kimmerman, I'm sure Hugh can recommend someone wonderful."

Hugh folded his arms across his chest. "*Interesting* is one word for it."

She kept her attention on Stanley. "Most power-tool consumers are men, and you, the manufacturers, are all competing for the same buyers. But imagine if *your* campaign was aimed at women. Bring in that market, and you're a leg up on the competition already."

Under his breath, Hugh mumbled something about ads in pink fonts, but not loudly enough to alienate his potential client. "We can certainly explore that idea if you're interested, Stanley, but I have to say, ignoring your target market is risky at best. Practically speaking, how many women do we think spend their disposable income on power tools?"

He turned to Joss, his eyebrows raised in an expression of mild curiosity. "*You*, for instance, just as a demographic example. Would you know the difference between a skill saw and a reciprocating saw?"

One of the fundamental rules of gunning for an account was demonstrating familiarity with the product, and everyone at the table knew Joss had never heard of Patone before today. Hugh's attempt to discredit her was simple, but delicately handled. An all-out assault on her credentials would seem like bullying, and besides, she sensed he saw her more as an annoyance than a real threat to be feared.

"No, I guess I'm not the reigning expert on saws. Or drills, or wrenches." Eyes innocently wide, she smiled at Hugh. "I admit it. When people think tool, you're what comes to mind."

He blinked, and she turned away quickly, appealing to Stanley. "But I did spend hours yesterday in home-improvement stores and can give you a female's perspective, if you're interested. I can also tell you that the popularity of home-makeover shows can be used to attract women."

She outlined a few of her thoughts, expounding on how and why women could be a valuable asset, especially when they were Christmas and birthday shopping for the men in their lives.

Vivian returned to the table, zipping her cell phone back into her purse. "What did I miss?"

Ever charming, Hugh rose to pull her chair out, but his smile was strained. "Joss has been sharing her...wonderful ideas."

Smiling inwardly, Joss cast a small sidelong glance in Hugh's direction. *Do you fear me now? Good.*

After the food arrived, all talk of anything requiring power cords and drill bits was put on hold, and Vivian genteelly monopolized conversation with real estate anecdotes. But when the check came, she reverted immediately to their earlier topic. "You should take Joss's card with you."

Joss almost flinched. As much as she wanted to succeed, especially if she beat Hugh in the process, there was something a little embarrassing about being twenty-eight and having your mother try to direct your business endeavors.

But Stanley was nodding. "I had already planned to ask. Young lady, you had some terrific ideas, and I'll be in touch with you this week."

Avoiding Hugh's gaze, she reached for her purse. Despite the few times this morning she'd wanted to cringe over Vivian's "help," Joss would be thrilled to have Stanley as a client. After everything that had happened in the past week—being told over a breakfast her agency had paid for that Neely-Richards was going with someone else, dealing with the EWA agent, not winning an ADster—Joss craved that adrenalized buzz of feeling like a winner.

"I'd love to hear from you," she told Stanley. "It was a pleasure meeting you."

She'd intended to tackle her kitchen wall today, but now she was torn. It ate at her to be surrounded by unfinished projects, but maybe her time was better spent researching and working up ideas for Patone instead. When Stanley called, she would be ready. What a coup it would be for Visions to sign him out from under Kimmerman!

Although Wyatt had assured her he wasn't disappointed with the second-place standing Friday night, her boss had been uncharacteristically subdued. Joss loathed the sensation of having let someone down, and this was her chance to make it up to him. She couldn't wait to get to work Monday morning.

In hindsight, she'd been in a slump lately, but her luck was about to change. She just knew it.

4

"WYATT, I HAVE GOOD NEWS!" Actually, what Joss had was more like a tentative lead, but why split hairs? Besides, she'd embraced the power of positive thinking.

Her boss lowered the coffee he'd been pouring into his Real Ad Men Get the Job Done in Under Thirty Seconds mug and gave her a wan smile. "Actually, I have some news of my own. Maybe I should go first."

Her breath caught. His mood lately *hadn't* been in her imagination. "What is it?"

"Let's talk in my office." Did he suggest that because they'd be more comfortable there, because no one arriving at work would walk in on the conversation, or because he was stalling?

She followed him past deserted cubicles. Joss was always among the first to arrive, but today, mocked at home by windows that needed new treatments and a kitchen decorated in Early Whorehouse, she'd left her place even earlier than usual. By the time she and Wyatt entered the glass-fronted presidential suite, she felt almost queasy with nerves.

"I was planning to tell the entire staff today, but maybe telling you first would be good practice," he said ominously, making her wonder if he suffered some ailment she didn't know about.

"There's something wrong?"

"Not technically. In fact, it's even good news."

Yeah, he looked like a man bursting at the seams with joy, what with the way he sighed heavily and fiddled with the container of pens on his desk instead of meeting her gaze. She lowered herself to the buttery-soft leather chair across from him and experienced a moment of déjà-dread. The knots in her stomach were tied in the same formations she'd felt when she watched a newscaster tell the city about Mitman's fraud.

Oh, God, surely she wasn't about to lose *another* job?

"I'm proud of Visions," he told her. "Proud of each of my employees, especially you. But I don't have your youth and energy, and I've been receiving buyout offers that are becoming more and more difficult to turn down. So Penelope and I decided to take one of them.... I'm retiring. I've worked hard over the last thirty years, and I've put in hours my wife was a saint to tolerate. But now we're going to spend time together before we get too old to make the most of it."

The words sank in slowly, in the same manner that water drained drop by excruciating drop in her clawfoot tub. "You *sold* Visions?"

"Legally, it's set up more as a merger—with me stepping down from the merged company. You, the staff, make Visions what it is, and you all have brand-new jobs waiting for you. With raises."

She liked the job she had. "And who will be paying these raises?"

"Kimmerman and Kimmerman."

Oh, no. Working for Hugh Brannon's employer? No, no, nooo.

Wyatt must have sensed her—*bone-deep hatred of the idea*—reluctance. "Joss, you're a talented young lady with a great career ahead of you. With your drive and ambition, you should be at a company like Kimmerman. They've got the resources to take you places."

"Mitman was a top company with prestige and national recognition, too." That had been one of the things that had drawn her to the position—even *Vivian* had been impressed. Until the slightly less impressive criminal suit.

Wyatt shook his head. "I know Rob Kimmerman and his son, and they're running an honest ship over there. Of course, I can't make you accept a job with them, but they'll need someone like you to ease the clients through the transitional period. And it'll be something of a transition for your colleagues, too."

Joss bit her lip. She didn't think Wyatt was trying to emotionally manipulate her, but she came preprogrammed with a sense of obligation to others' expectations. She didn't want to fail him. Besides, smart women didn't voluntarily chunk their incomes when the ink on their mortgage papers wasn't quite dry.

A raise would certainly make it easier to refit her kitchen with a stove *not* off by sixty degrees and wallpaper that didn't say "hourly charge includes condoms." Then there was the new water heater she needed, the sink that needed to be replaced in the laundry room so that she wasn't in danger of a small domestic flood every time she ran a load of darks, her bedroom floor upstairs that dipped ominously if you stepped beneath the ceiling fan…

"When are you telling everyone else?" she asked, trying to get her bearings.

"Staff meeting first thing this morning. I hope you don't think me too selfish, Joss, but Penelope and I can't pass up this opportunity. And I really think it's what's best for all of you, too."

She forced a smile for the man who had taken her under his wing when she joined the firm. "I've always trusted your judgment."

His shoulders sagged with relief. "Then you'll help me get everyone else excited about the idea?"

What? "Oh. Of course." That should be quite the pep talk.

Still, if she'd somehow been able to convince herself she truly wanted to live in a house that would make Bob Vila turn and run screaming into the street, then surely she could convince a handful of people they wanted to work with Hu—er, Kimmerman and Kimmerman.

HUGH STEPPED INSIDE Kimmerman Sr.'s office, a spacious suite that overlooked a putting green and boasted its own executive washroom. On the other side of the mahogany desk, Robert Kimmerman held up a finger to signal his almost being finished with an e-mail, and Hugh sat down to wait. When he'd arrived that morning, his phone had already been blinking with voice mail from the company's president. Hugh doubted the older man wanted to see him "immediately" to congratulate him again on the ADster win. Was this a status check on Patone Power Tools?

Until yesterday, Hugh would have bet money on his sitting here now with a contract signed by Stanley Patone…and Hugh almost never lost a bet. But he hadn't factored in Joss McBride as an obstacle.

Her appearance at the restaurant yesterday morning had completely blindsided him. He told himself the surprise he'd felt was why he'd been so off-kilter throughout the brunch—not because he was preoccupied with thoughts of courting *her* instead of the prospective client.

Watching her walk toward him in the familiar setting, catching the spicy fragrance of her tantalizing perfume, battling her for an account...it had been just like old times, except without the hot sex. Which was like braving the traffic to reach the stadium, getting all revved up during the pregame activities and then leaving before the kickoff. He hadn't been able to stop thinking about her once he finally climbed into bed that night and tried to sleep. He didn't actually mind the dreams she'd inspired, but he wondered if she'd thought about him, too. Missed him?

Even if she had, billboard companies would be giving away free ad space downtown before she ever admitted it.

The clacking of keys stopped, and Robert sat back in his tall leather chair. "Sorry to keep you waiting, just wanted to send that off while I had the wording perfect in my mind. Now, I suppose you're wondering what the urgent matter is."

"Patone Power Tools?"

The older man pshawed that suggestion. "Stanley contacted *us*—it's not as though we had to seek him out and win him over. And with you on it, his business is a done deal."

Hugh coughed.

He'd spent yesterday afternoon redoubling his efforts for marketing strategies, certain Joss was home doing the same thing. But then he'd realized that an hour with her had catapulted him instantly back into past competitive habits. He'd spent Friday night at the ADsters, come into the office for a few hours on Saturday, then taken a business brunch Sunday morning. Didn't he deserve a few weekend hours that were his own? He'd concluded that he was justified—*obligated*, even—to push aside his work and turn on the football game. Yet somehow, he couldn't see himself presenting that argument now to the boss seated opposite him who considered Patone "a done deal."

Hugh was relieved when Kimmerman continued without asking how brunch had gone. Hugh would eventually tell him about the possible competition from Visions, of course, but it was rude to interrupt.

"I want to talk about something much more exciting," Kimmerman said. "I'd hoped Robbie would be here for the announcement, but he won't be back from New York until midweek."

Despite having worked here for a year, Hugh still had trouble thinking of the forty-something vice president as "Robbie." He supposed it was better than calling the VP Junior, though technically Robbie was "the third." Father and son were alike in everything from wardrobe to client philosophy, and they would've passed for brothers if not for a few additional wrinkles around Kimmerman Sr.'s hazel eyes and the silver in his dark hair.

"I got final word this weekend..." The older man stopped in one of those dramatic pauses that are usually more annoying than theatrical. "Kimmerman and Kimmerman is acquiring Wyatt Allen's Group. We're merging with Visions!"

Merging? With Joss?

Only in the business sense, Hugh reminded himself, blinking. "When did this happen? Never mind. I know you said over the weekend, I'm just—"

"Surprised," Kimmerman said, looking pleased with himself. "We weren't sure Wyatt would accept the offer, and the last thing we wanted was to stir up other agencies' interest in making the same acquisition. But we dotted all the *i*'s and crossed the *t*'s with our lawyers on Saturday. He'll be letting his people know today."

Since she'd been on his mind all night, Hugh couldn't help but think of Joss. What would her reaction be?

"How exactly will the merger work?" Hugh wanted to know. "Will there be layoffs, or—"

"Not at all. Their staff isn't big enough to make positions truly redundant, but the people they do employ are superb. Jocelyn McBride, in particular. She has a track record nearly as impressive as yours, but I'm sure you already know all about her. One of the reasons I wanted you to be among the first to know is I understand you and Ms. McBride used to—"

An image of Joss naked and smiling flashed through Hugh's mind.

"—work together."

Oh. *Work.* Yeah, they'd done that, too.

Hugh nodded. "I know Joss pretty well."

"Good, good. I'll be counting on you two to help me integrate the staffs. The sooner we overlap job functions and client lists, the sooner we eliminate any 'us, them' mentalities. I'm going to have some sort of employee-appreciation event immediately, welcome the new people and encourage everyone to get to know each other. In fact, maybe you could even have lunch or dinner with Ms. McBride this week, lay the foundation for when the people from Visions move into the office."

Actually, that foundation had been pretty well laid, and Kimmerman had as much chance of successfully building on it as a construction crew did on quicksand. Nonetheless, Hugh grinned at the thought of calling Joss to ask her out—should prove entertaining, if not productive. And, if they were going to be working together again, he definitely planned to have some fun with it. He wasn't going to let her turn him into a heart attack in a pair of loafers.

ALL DAY MONDAY, Joss wanted to phone Emily, but she couldn't risk being overheard, not when Wyatt was trusting her to help soothe any alarm her coworkers might be feeling. Declaring to Em that Wyatt had lost his mind and sold out to the enemy might not enhance office morale.

Joss had dutifully gone to lunch with Nick and Cherie for pizza and panic. Nick wondered if his conservative persona would damage his creative credibility with people who didn't know him, and Cherie lamented that despite the promised job security, she was the most expendable person in the merged companies. Kimmerman, after all, already had a receptionist.

Now that the Day that Wouldn't End finally had, Joss was home and free to vent, rather than reassure.

She went upstairs to change into a pair of jeans and a baggy sweater and saw that the answering machine on her nightstand was blinking. Funny how the flashing red light somehow always made a message seem urgent, even when it was just a misplaced call for Bob.

She hit Play, her index finger hovering right above the erase button in case it was a salesperson—or worse, a recorded mechanical pitch from a robo-salesperson.

"Hi, Joss." Hugh Brannon's whisky-smooth tone filled her bedroom, and she almost deleted him in an involuntary muscle spasm. What was he doing, calling her to gloat? She really should have forked over the extra dough for an unlisted number.

"This is Hugh, but I'm guessing you already knew that. Just heard the good news...Brannon and McBride together again."

Grinding her teeth, she pressed Stop. McBride was doing just fine without Brannon. She'd listen to the rest of the message later, after she'd talked to Emily and possibly blended a pitcher of Today Sucks Margaritas. Although, until the electrician came next week to look at the wiring, she had to plug her blender and other small kitchen appliances into outlets in the living room.

She plopped down on the comforter of her neatly made bed and grabbed the cordless phone from its base. Truthfully, by late afternoon, she'd begun to calm down—Wyatt's deal *did* provide increased salaries and benefits, as well as corporate budgets that would allow people like her and Nick to flex their creative muscles more—but hearing Hugh's voice had disrupted her newfound inner peace. Maybe in a company the size of Kimmerman, they wouldn't even run into each other, she told herself in an attempt at positive thinking.

She jabbed in the last digits of Emily's number and listened to the phone ring.

"Hello?" Emily didn't sound like herself.

It took Joss a moment of mental processing to realize her friend's greeting had actually been "Hel-*sniff*-lo?"

A cold, maybe? "Hey, Em. Is this a bad time?"

"N-not at a-all." Sniff, sniff.

Suddenly Joss forgot all about her own day. "Emily, are you okay?"

That, as it turned out, had been the wrong thing to ask.

The sniffling deteriorated into incoherent sobs. There were words in there somewhere, but darned if Joss could understand any of them. Her chest tightened as she waited, wanting to help her friend but not yet knowing what emergency might require her assistance.

"It's S-simon," Emily finally got out.

I'll kill him. Finding out what he'd actually done was irrelevant. Unless…oh dear, had something happened *to* him, and that's why Emily was upset? "What happened?"

"He accepted a job up north," Emily said. "It's with a good school, and I would've been h-happy for him, honest, but he was just so eager to go… He s-said he'd only been marking time here. That there w-wasn't anything in his life here he cared about."

Ouch.

"Oh, Em." Was this an insensitive time to tell her friend she was better off without the condescending rat bastard? Probably it was more appropriate to console now, Simon-bash later.

"You're better off without the condescending rat

bastard." All right, she wasn't perfect. God knows she was working on it.

"But he was smart and s-self-assured."

Try self-involved.

"Joss, he looked at me like…well, okay, half of the time he looked at me like some kind of unpaid research assistant, but *other* times, he looked at me like a woman. It was flattering. You've seen some of the losers I attract."

Joss's heart constricted into a pained ball for her friend. "I'm sure lots of guys would love to be with you. You probably didn't notice any of them checking you out when you were with Simon because you were so faithful to him."

There was a nasal sound—either a snort of disbelief, or Emily blowing her nose. "You don't understand, Joss. I *know* Simon wasn't Prince Charming, but he was…better than being alone. You broke up with David. Hugh, too. The truth is, you could have a guy if you really wanted one. Me—"

"Emily Gruber, you stop it right there!"

Joss knew all about feeling inadequate. How often had she brought home an A, only to end up guilt stricken that it hadn't been an A plus? Hell, just last week she'd been torturing herself with what she could've done differently to win the Neely-Richards account.

"Sorry," Emily said after a pause, sounding marginally more like herself. "He was driving away right when you called, so I was pretty much in the throes of self-pity."

"No apology needed. If you want to cry, I'm here to listen, just don't beat yourself up." Beating up

Simon was definitely preferable. The man deserved to be smacked in the head with the hardcover version of his published thesis.

Emily cleared her throat. "Unless you're psychic, this isn't why you called. Is there something—?"

"Unimportant," Joss said loyally. Well, it was fifty-one percent loyalty and forty-nine percent not wanting to think about the fact that as early as next week she'd be working with Hugh Brannon. But, hey, fifty-one was technically a majority. "My thing can wait if you need to talk."

"No. I think I dwelled on him enough while we were together. If the man's leaving, I'm going to move on. I won't give him the satisfaction of obsessing over him."

"Good for you! Wanna not obsess at my place? I'll make Men Suck Margaritas." Similar to the Today Sucks variety, but less lime, more triple sec. "Come on, misery loves tequila. You can give me your input on the dining-room border while you're here."

"Aha! You're trying to draft me into renovations. I show up, you hand me a can of spackle and tell me nothing gets the mind off an ex like some light labor?"

Joss laughed. "If there's one thing I've learned it's that renovations are heavy labor. Besides, if I thought for a second that working on the house would make me forget—" She bit her lip, but not soon enough.

"Make *you* forget? I thought I was the one who needed to block an ex from her mind."

How did the old ads go—the ones about the phone service that was so good you could hear a pin drop? Joss's current connection was clear enough she could actually hear the whisper of her friend's ears perking up.

"Joss, you wouldn't be so cruel as to withhold juicy info in my time of dire need?"

"Kimmerman is buying Visions. Bought, actually. Over the weekend. Effective immediately. By next week, I'll be working with Hugh again."

"Ohmigosh! Hugh? Your Hugh?"

"*No.* Well, yes, Hugh Brannon, but—"

"Wow. That's…wow. Are you okay?"

Emily sounded almost comically concerned, as if she worried that Joss was standing on a ledge somewhere even as they spoke. Which was ridiculous, because if Joss ventured out onto the old-fashioned ledge of her bedroom window, she'd no doubt crash into the oak trees below.

"I'm fine," Joss said. "The man is a pain in my ass, but the situation isn't, as you might put it, dire. Still, the one bright spot in the whole Mitman fiasco was my not having to work with him anymore, and now… If you'd like to come over, I was serious about those margaritas."

There was a pause as Emily deliberated. "Maybe I should take a rain check. I would love to hang out, but I'm feeling pretty drained. Then again, if I don't drive to your place, it's either grade research proposals or sit here feeling guilty because I should be grading research proposals. Give me a few minutes to wash my face and cut Simon's picture into tiny pieces, and I'll call you back if I'm feeling up to it."

"I'll be here," Joss promised. In the meantime, if she needed to vent, she had her cat. Siamese were extremely vocal, so Dulcie always had something to say.

Of course, the spayed cat held a rather narrow perspective on gender relations, her experience limited to once swatting the nose of a tom with amorous intentions.

In light of today's news, Joss hadn't brought home any work with her—would her clients even be hers a month from now?—and restlessness gnawed at her. She didn't want to start something she couldn't finish if Emily came over, but she didn't want to waste a valuable opportunity to make progress, either. Carrying the cordless with her, she went downstairs to feed Dulcie, trying to ignore the dining room that screamed for a new paint job and the foyer linoleum she needed to replace.

She'd bought the house with high enthusiasm for bringing out its true potential, yet she hadn't realized how difficult she'd find living inside a work in progress. There was so much to do that sometimes being here was a little overwhelming to a struggling perfectionist. As she was pitching the small emptied can of cat food into the trash, the phone rang. Thank God.

"Tell me you called to take me up on my offer," Joss said without preamble, knowing she had neither the time to affect serious change tonight nor the patience to just relax in her living room.

"Well, that depends," said a very amused, very male voice. "Exactly what offer would that be?"

5

"HUGH." JOSS CLEARED HER THROAT, glad he couldn't see her blush. "Hi. I, um, obviously thought you were someone else."

"Obviously," he agreed, his killer smile evident in his voice. "The intriguing question is, who?"

"None of your business." She said it with a light wouldn't-you-like-to-know air that hinted at her having mysterious lovers and exciting plans. No need to admit her choices for the evening were to hang out with Emily, a chick flick DVD playing in the background; or attack the final layer of kitchen wallpaper with a putty knife, a watchful Dulcie wondering why Joss didn't just use her claws.

"Did you happen to get my message earlier?" He didn't give her a chance to answer before adding, "I was surprised that your number's changed."

"I moved. Your invitation to the housewarming must've been lost in the mail."

He laughed. "With you in the office, I'm going to have to start wearing armor to work."

At the reminder that they'd soon be working together, she sank into one of the chairs at the kitchen table. It wasn't fair that he always seemed to have seniority over her. He'd been hired at Mitman just a month ahead of her, and now she'd be the new kid on his block at Kimmerman. It was a wonder she'd never given more serious thought to going off and opening her own agency. Guaranteed Hugh-free.

"Maybe we won't actually be spending a lot of time together," she said tentatively. "You're always pointing out what a big company it is."

"Boy, are you in for a disappointment," he warned. "Kimmerman's putting you and me unofficially in charge of the transition. He thinks getting everyone to play nicely works better when it comes from within the ranks instead of management, and given our past history…"

Past history? He probably wasn't referring to the part where she'd racked her brain to come up with a winning campaign and had said something off-the-cuff to her lover, who'd used it to generate a great idea and win her client.

"So, I was calling to see if you wanted to grab dinner or something," he concluded. "Get reacquainted."

The playful note of invitation in his voice did not slide along her nerve endings in a warm caress, she told herself. The man *grated* on her nerves. Big difference. Any suggestion that her body had tensed expectantly in her seat or that she'd briefly closed her eyes and took a moment to remember his…acquaintance…was a vicious lie spread by her cat.

She kept her tone crisp and businesslike. "Actually, my schedule's pretty full this week. But we're both professionals. I'm sure office hours will be enough time to take care of whatever needs to be done."

"No problem." He sounded unsurprised by her refusal. "I'd just as soon spend the evening polishing my PowerPoint presentation. I have a meeting with Stanley Patone in the morning."

Damn. She'd been so poleaxed by Wyatt's news today she'd forgotten all about Stanley and his promise to get in touch with her. Would her new boss simply ask her to leave Patone to Hugh?

"With us playing on the same team now," Hugh added, as though he were reading her thoughts, "my winning the account is like a victory for both of us."

Maybe Dulcie was on to something with her swat-'em-on-the-nose approach to males. "The same could be said about *my* getting the account," Joss said sweetly.

"Right," he said, sounding as if he was as worried about that possibility as he was about an asteroid suddenly crashing through his roof and thunking him in the head. "I guess I'll see you next week, then. Unless you change your mind about us getting together?"

When the devil takes up ice hockey. "See you Monday. I'm looking forward to our working together," she added in her most polished tone. He didn't need to know she'd glanced down to make sure her pants hadn't caught fire.

Once they'd disconnected, she realized she was even more restless than before. Definitely time to take care of this bordello-red kitchen once and for all. She stood, wielding her putty knife with menace.

Ever since the day she'd met him, Hugh Brannon had managed to come out ahead in every situation, whether he charmed or schemed his way to the winning position. She didn't deny that he was good at his job, but he was ridiculously lucky, too. The State Lottery Commission probably had some kind of legal ban against his buying tickets. And then there was *her*...somehow managing to sign on with the one agency in the area that Hugh's employer decided to take over.

Well, Joss was going to apply herself one hundred and ten percent at Kimmerman, and for a change, Hugh would see *her* on top. Figuratively speaking.

KIMMERMAN AND KIMMERMAN was housed in one of those shiny downtown skyscrapers that was all windows and mirrored modern beauty that caught the setting sun's reflection and blinded interstate drivers during rush hour. Visions had leased space in a one-story building with a few parking spaces out front and a shared lot in the back. Now, her first day at Kimmerman, Joss punched in a code at the bottom of a winding garage, then followed the speed bumps up the different levels, until she finally managed to snag a space on the sixth floor near the elevators.

The past week had been a blur, with Kimmerman Sr. coming to the office—her former office—several times to meet the Visions staff and familiarize himself with the work being done for their more important clients. Joss suspected mergers weren't usually executed so swiftly, but with the decision made and the paperwork signed, Wyatt had no desire to draw out the transition, watching everything he'd built up pass into another man's hands. No, he and Penelope would rather be in Aruba.

Visions was a small company, and relocating wasn't that complicated. Still, Cherie and one or two other employees would stay behind for a couple of weeks to redirect business and "tie up loose ends," while Joss and Nick came to Kimmerman immediately to "get the ball rolling." Kimmerman, Joss had learned quickly, was fond of clichés.

Last week had been busy outside of work, as well. Her kitchen, except for one resistant patch above her sink, now sported a wallpaper of muted yellows and blues. The electrician had also stopped by to work his wiring magic, and he'd assured her she could plug the toaster into a kitchen outlet without having to worry about toast—or, big plus, herself—being shot across the room. Her stove and new laundry-room sink were on back order, and the plumber, who was going to replace her water heater, had told her that although he couldn't commit to a specific time tomorrow, she could expect him between 9 a.m. and March.

Then there had been the shopping trip with Emily over the weekend, when her friend had asked for assistance finding a new guy.

"You were right all along about Simon," Emily had said as they rode up the escalator in their favorite department store. "Maybe I should let you pick my next boyfriend."

Joss hadn't admitted that she'd been giving the matter thought since before Simon's departure and might have to find Dulcie a new vet, since Dr. Dan had seemed unconvinced when she'd explained she wasn't hitting on him. "I'll be happy to help."

Now, as Joss pulled her briefcase out of the passenger seat and locked her midsize sedan behind her, she wondered if there were any potential dates for

Emily working here at Kimmerman. Surely not all the men were like Hugh.

She pressed the button for the elevator. Actually...she'd never met *any* man quite like Hugh.

Moments later, she found herself standing in a marble-floored hallway, staring at a brass sign that welcomed her to her future: Kimmerman and Kimmerman Advertising Specialists. She strode toward the door, chin up, briefcase in hand, the heels of her best professional pumps clicking on the tile.

Inside the carpeted reception area, which was home to several posh white sofas and black glass tables, Joss was greeted by the smiling redhead who sat behind a curved counter. "Welcome to Kimmerman and Kimmerman. May I help you?"

"Maybe. I'm Jocelyn McBride, from Visions."

"Of course. It's nice to meet you." The young woman, whom Joss estimated to be around twenty-three or twenty-four, stood and reached across the counter to shake Joss's hand. "I'm Lydia. Lydia Jenkins. Mr. Kimmerman asked me to keep an eye out for you. He'd like to see you once you get your bearings. One of your fellow Visions co-workers got in a few minutes ago. Nick?"

Joss nodded. Normally, she'd marvel at the oddity of his beating her to work, but she knew from his reaction last week that he was nervous.

The other woman lowered her voice to a confidential whisper. "Cute—strange leather pants, but cute. Is he seeing anyone?"

"Not that I'm aware of," Joss said, trying not to laugh at the idea of Nick in his "creative costume."

Emily aside, it seemed Kimmerman held dating

potential for at least one of her friends. *This is your career, Jocelyn, not* The Love Boat. The sharp voice in her head sounded annoyingly like Vivian's, but that didn't make the words any less true. Joss had other things to think about than matchmaking.

Lydia rounded the high reception desk. "Here, I'll point you in the right direction. Phones are generally dead for another few minutes, anyway."

Joss followed, grateful for the impromptu tour. The front of the office space was given to conference rooms and presentation areas for clients. The departments that took care of in-house concerns like accounting, human resources and IT all worked to the right of the reception area, and the account execs and creatives were housed to the left.

In some big agencies, the account reps and creative teams stayed as far away from each other as possible, in conflict with each other half the time despite a seemingly common goal. Execs were worried about things like keeping difficult clients happy, even when it meant the graphics people had to go back to the drawing board three or four times. And the creative geniuses wanted time to perfect their vision, while ad reps wanted to promise everything to the customer immediately.

But here at Kimmerman, the two departments worked together closely and were encouraged to brainstorm marketing approaches together. Joss and Nick actually had a good background for this format, since the small staff at Visions had frequently had overlapping job descriptions.

"You'll be in here somewhere," Lydia said, stopping in a back corner of the building. A modest desk unofficially marked the border of Exectopia, and a brass-and-wood nameplate reading Annette Clarion presided between the computer and phone. Beyond the vacant desk was floor space carved up into mauve-walled cubicles, like once-open pastureland that had been dissected into hamster habitats. Beyond *that* were the outer offices for the stiffs lucky enough to rate them.

"I'm the main receptionist," Lydia said, "but Annette fields calls for reps when it gets busy and makes sure nothing slips by if one of you are traveling. She acts as the general administrative assistant for this department—handles reservations, expense reports, setting up meetings. She started in the steno pool when Robert, Sr. was the junior in Kimmerman and Kimmerman. Great at her job."

After a quick glance around, Lydia added under her breath, "But she's a battle-ax and holds a grudge, not that you heard it from me."

Joss nodded crisply, filing away the information.

"Hugh Brannon's probably the one to give you more specifics on what goes on back here," Lydia said, suddenly grinning broadly. "Talk about cute!"

Oh, let's not and say we did. And it just figured that Hugh was being referenced as the man to see—he'd barely worked here a year! "You don't think I should speak to someone who's been around a little longer?"

"Nah. We lost our top guy to Madison Avenue a few months ago and one of our top gals to the joys of motherhood. Hugh distinguished himself pretty quickly."

"Stop, I'm blushing," Hugh said from behind them.

Joss actually jumped. Maybe, she thought as she

turned to face him, she could get him to wear some kind of little bell around his neck. Hey, it kept Dulcie from sneaking up on her.

"Hugh. Good morning."

His memorably kissable lips curved into a grin as he gave her body a lazy once-over. "Yes, it is. Just got better in fact. Nice to see you again, Joss."

The weird part was he sounded as if he meant it.

Joss realized for the first time that he was carrying his laptop case and a handful of folders. Was he only just now arriving? The Hugh she'd been involved with was usually the first to show up—except of course on the mornings she'd managed to beat him, which was why he tried so hard to be early. Neither of them enjoyed second place.

Today, especially, she'd expected him to be ensconced in his office and an air of superiority. *She* would've come in earlier, but it seemed silly to do so when she wouldn't even have a work space of her own until somebody assigned her one.

Lydia's exhale was more like a dreamy sigh. "I should probably get back to man the phones. It was nice to meet you, Joss, but I'm sure Hugh can take it from here." Then the receptionist turned down the carpeted corridor.

Hugh's smile became suddenly wry. "I'd invite you to the break room to get a cup of coffee with me, but somehow I doubt time alone with me is high on your list of priorities."

She'd rather scoop Dulcie's kitty litter box. "Don't be silly. I'm a professional, and we're going to be working together. Spending time with you doesn't faze me at all." Unless you counted her pulse accelerating and the way she couldn't help but notice his richly sensual cologne.

"Come on." He inclined his head toward the untamed frontier beyond the cubicles, where one might still dream of a window. "I'll show you to your office."

She was relieved to have one. He preceded her into a linoleum-floored space with overhead fluorescent lighting and a small window with black miniblinds. Since the blinds were currently closed, the view below could be anything from a gurgling picturesque fountain to an industrial-size trash bin.

"This is nice," she said, setting her briefcase atop the smooth mahogany desk. What the room lacked in spaciousness, it made up for in state-of-the-art furnishings, including a sleek silver PC and an office chair that looked comfy enough to encourage people to work late. As if she'd ever needed to be coaxed to put forth extra effort.

He nodded. "Not bad at all. A lot like my office...except, of course, mine's bigger."

Did the man stand in front of his mirror at home and practice goading her, or did she just somehow provoke him into comments like that?

"I don't mind something cozy." She smiled. "Women's self-worth isn't all tied up in size."

He threw his head back and laughed, the simple pleasure he was taking in their time together an aphrodisiac of sorts. *Stop right there,* she warned herself. *This is how it started before, remember?* They'd exchanged little quips, then kisses, and the next thing she'd known, he had her in bed and had the promotion she'd wanted. She was brand-new here, needed to prove herself. She *didn't* need the distraction of Hugh Brannon.

"So which direction is Kimmerman's office?" she asked.

Hugh raised an eyebrow at the edge in her voice. "A little nervous about our spending time like this *mano a mano?*" Lowering his gaze, he did another one of those once-overs that made her abdomen tighten in a knot of desire. "Or *mano a* womano."

She sighed. "It doesn't mean 'man to man.'" For a moment, she'd almost been able to feel his *manos* on her, and the sensation was a bittersweet one.

Joss had grown up living with a person who made her feel never quite good enough. Did she really want to be involved with someone she was always competing with, someone who often subjected her to that same "close, but not quite" emotion?

"I know what it means, J." His voice was softer than usual, but seemed to carry across her new office all the more because of it. "As long as we're on definitions, though, you should look up *joke* sometime. You could stand to laugh more."

With that, he spun on his heel.

I laugh. They hadn't broken up because she lacked a sense of humor. She'd broken things off with him when he'd not only stolen the account she'd been working on tirelessly, but edged her out of a promotion without even acknowledging how important it had been to her. Granted, maybe she could have—ack! Five minutes with the man, and she was already questioning herself? Analyzing how she could have done things better?

She followed after him, waiting as he discarded his belongings in his office, which was indeed larger than hers. Hugh was no good for her. A man with dimples like that wasn't good for *any* woman, but the other women of the world were going to have to look out for themselves.

Two hours later, however, it had been made depressingly clear to Joss that she and Hugh were stuck together for the immediate future. After Hugh had shown her to Kimmerman Sr.'s office, a posh suite redolent with the faint fragrance of pipe tobacco, the president of the company had enthusiastically outlined his plans for Hugh and Joss working together.

"I want there to be some crossover between the two companies' clients and execs," the man had said.

Well, of course he did—if this merger didn't take and Joss went elsewhere, he didn't want her spiriting away her Visions accounts with her. But nobody brought up that aspect of company politics.

"You two, with your prior work history, are a good place to start. Make sure the customers that started with Wyatt feel they're getting the same treatment as the accounts we've had with us for years," the stately man instructed them. "Jocelyn, I've selected one or two clients in your portfolio that I'd like you to bring Hugh up to speed on."

She hadn't been here a day and a half and she was losing customers she'd recruited to Hugh? That had to be some kind of record.

"And, Hugh, by bringing Joss in on a couple of the projects you have in the works, people will get to see the ever evolving face of K and K. I was thinking, for instance, that she could try cracking the Weavers, since you haven't been able to get as firm a commitment from them as we'd hoped."

Hugh tensed almost imperceptibly in the chair next to her, and Joss suddenly felt ten pounds lighter. *Hugh* had been striking out with someone? Glory be. She liked these Weavers already.

Weaver Investing, Kimmerman explained, was interested in signing with an agency, but they were— to put it delicately—"exacting clients."

"'Exacting,'" Hugh muttered as they left their boss's office after the long meeting, "doesn't begin to cover it. Those people have no sense of humor and entirely too much money."

"Sure you're not just bitter because they didn't want to turn that money over to you?" Joss asked.

"You can quit grinning like that." He turned toward the corner of the building where their offices were. "What makes you think you'll fare any better? They're impossible to please."

Watch me. "Maybe they're just discerning."

"Imagine the most anal-retentive number cruncher you can, but without the warmth and fun-loving personality. And that *still* wouldn't be as bad as Janice Weaver and her husband. But, hey, more power to you. I'll ask Annette to set up dinner or something with them this week."

Joss shot him a suspicious sidelong glance. Had he mellowed since their doomed affair? The Hugh she'd known, after losing an opportunity to her, wouldn't have rested without getting in the last word.

The cubicled area they'd left earlier was now bustling with strange faces that belonged to names she needed to learn—starting with the dour-faced woman sitting behind the desk. *I've seen her before.*

Just as Hugh was introducing silver-haired Annette Clarion, recognition clicked. The administrative assistant Joss would be working with on a daily basis was the woman from the restroom at the ADster awards, the one who hadn't appreciated Joss's colorful language. Judging from her pursed lips, Annette hadn't forgotten the encounter, either.

Damn. At least she'd managed not to say it out loud.

"Nice to meet you," Joss said.

"Likewise," the woman answered, despite her I've-been-sucking-raw-lemons expression.

"I was just telling Jocelyn that you could help her set up something with the Weavers this week," Hugh said. "Maybe yet another fine meal on the company's tab will convince these people to go with us."

Joss was buoyed by his frustration, but not because she was evil and took pleasure in his suffering. Not entirely, anyway. It was just so refreshing to see him not immediately succeed at something. He'd never been more attractive than he was at that moment, his full lips twisted slightly in a scowl she was tempted to kiss away.

Whoa! Hold the phone there, girlfriend.

Reminding herself that her goal here was the Weavers and not seducing Hugh into a better mood, she told him in a light, confident tone, "Don't worry about wishing me luck. I won't need it."

"You're probably right. As uptight and demanding as they are, you should be a perfect match." Then, having scored that last word, he turned toward his office.

And to think she'd been worried he'd softened into a kinder, gentler Hugh.

6

CALL HER A PESSIMIST, but Joss couldn't shake the feeling that a business dinner that ended with a trip to the emergency room did not equal success.

Groaning, she leaned back in the uncomfortable green plastic chair in the waiting room, staring sightlessly at the muted television overhead in the corner opposite her. Her temples were throbbing in the beginnings of a migraine, but she counted herself lucky to have merely the headache from hell and not Janice Weaver's roiling stomach. Joss had been so intent on giving her presentation that she hadn't had time to eat the apparently tainted seafood hors d'oeuvres. At the moment, she felt more guilty than grateful.

Janice and her husband weren't in any danger and would no doubt be fine in a day or so, but the woman's discomfort had been enough to send them seeking medical help. All because of the restaurant Joss had picked—painstakingly, no less. She'd gone out of her way to research Janice Weaver's tastes and find a unique setting in which they could meet. Some place Hugh never would have thought to take them.

Congratulations. He probably wouldn't have come up with County General. Also, she'd no doubt succeeded in her goal of making an unforgettable impression on the Weavers. She'd accompanied them to the emergency room, figuring that moral support and helping fill out paperwork were the least she could do for the couple, who were now back with the on-call doctor.

Her first big assignment for Kimmerman, and she'd blown it spectacularly. After her hours of prep on Monday and Tuesday—planning what she'd say, carefully selecting a restaurant—she could have produced better results by ad-libbing a pitch at the drive-through window of a fast-food burger chain. This was not how it was supposed to work.

She'd called Kimmerman earlier to apprise him of the situation. Now she needed a friendly ear. She dug her cell phone out of her purse. As much as she'd encouraged Em to get out there and meet guys who weren't Simon, at the moment, Joss hoped her friend was home.

"Hello?"

Oh, good. At least one of Joss's wishes for the evening hadn't been mocked by the cosmos. "Emily, I'm so glad you're there."

"Hey! How'd it go?"

Joss had promised to call her friend with details of the dinner and presentation, but she hadn't planned on doing so in a waiting room filled with magazines circa 1982, beneath an intercom speaker that seemed to page a different doctor every three minutes.

"We'd barely made it into the entrees when my client—prospective client, anyway. *Former* prospective client... Oh, hell."

"That bad?" Emily asked, sounding startled.

Yes, actually. But Joss's muttered curse had more

to do with the dark-haired man striding through the automatic sliding doors at the front of the waiting room. What was Hugh doing here?

A pained groan escaped her, and a nurse looked out from behind the registration window. "Hang in there, miss. Someone will be with you as soon as possible."

Joss didn't even bother to correct her—at the moment, she *did* feel ill.

Hugh's eyes met hers, and he slowed his stride, as if taking the extra time to figure out what to say. Funny, she would've thought pointing and laughing pretty much covered it. He certainly hadn't hesitated in the last few days to make jokes at her expense. What bothered her was that some of them had actually been amusing, but she didn't need Robert Kimmerman to view her as a source of comic relief, or, worse, ridicule.

"Em, I'm sorry to dial and run, but I'm gonna need to call you back."

"As soon as possible. I'm dying of curiosity!"

Joss disconnected and glanced up at Hugh. "Kimmerman send you to make sure I didn't accidentally kill off the client?"

His lips twitched. "You really think there's any chance left that they're going to become clients?"

No. She'd just finished admitting as much, but voicing her failure to Hugh was different. She'd rather tell her mother what had happened.

"Relax, it was my idea to come." Hugh shrugged out of his lightweight trench coat and sat in the ugly little chair next to her. "Robert Jr. got back from an important business trip this afternoon, and I was having dinner with him and his father when you called."

Well, if he'd been using the time with the agency's owners to sharpen the edge he had over Joss, he needn't have bothered.

"When Robert told us what happened, I thought maybe you could use a friend." Then he grinned. "But since I didn't know how to get a hold of any of your friends, I came instead."

His unexpected comment surprised a laugh out of her, and at the short burst, several people looked up from their clipboards of insurance forms and patient information.

Hugh smiled approvingly. "Glad I was able to get you to laugh. That was Plan A."

He gave her upper arm a brief, encouraging squeeze, then unexpectedly moved his fingers to the area between her shoulder and neck. She should move away from the unprofessional contact, but the gently kneading massage was the best thing that had happened to her all night. "Plan B was to go to the pharmacy and beg for some kind of sedative on your behalf. I figured you'd be through the roof."

"Please, I'm here representing our employer. I handle crises with aplomb." She flashed a rueful smile. "But I was planning to go home and eat about two gallons of ice cream once the crisis was over."

No sooner had the words left her mouth than a memory hit her, and a blush tingled in her cheeks. She could tell from the way Hugh's fingers suddenly stilled and his gaze heated that he was thinking about the same thing. When they were dating, they'd had a "working weekend" at his apartment, but spent a lot of it in bed—Hugh insisted sex made him creative, and she could certainly attest to that. It had been almost two in the morning when they'd decided they needed sustenance, long after the Waif had closed for the night and take-out places had stopped delivering.

He hadn't had much in the way of groceries, but they'd found butter-pecan ice cream. She could taste the rich flavor, hear their laughter as melting drops fell on his sheets as they fed each other. And, against all good judgment, she could definitely feel the freezing, fleeting sensation of ice cream on her skin before Hugh licked it away, the contrast of cold against her heated body becoming increasingly erotic. That had been the weekend she'd realized she was falling in love with him.

He'd won the Stefan's Salons account a week later. The second memory wasn't nearly as pleasurable as the first, and she stiffened, signaling with her tensed muscles that now would be a good time for him to stop touching her.

"If you came to offer your support, I appreciate it, but I'm fine. And if you came to do damage control and save the account, you might want to wait until Mrs. Weaver is feeling a little better."

He cocked his head to the side. "You think signing the client was my first thought?"

Um...*duh.* "Since when is that not your first thought?"

Frowning, he opened his mouth, then closed it and leaned back in his chair. "I was actually at this same hospital a few months ago."

"I'm guessing not because you tried to poison anyone with a seafood appetizer?"

"My brother Craig had a heart attack."

"Oh." *Nice time to be flippant, McBride.* She leaned forward, covering the hand she'd shrugged away just moments ago. "I'm sorry. Is he—"

"He's okay. Trying to learn to take things a little slower and not learning as fast as the rest of the family would like, but physically, he's recovered. You know he's only a few years older than I am? And in great shape. The man plays squash with the D.A. every week."

Hugh was in pretty spectacular shape, too, but she could hear the uncharacteristic vulnerability underlying his bewildered tone. He was thinking that if it could happen to Craig, it could happen to him. She experienced a moment of unguarded tenderness.

"And you?" she asked. "Are you okay?"

"Me? I'm great. But if you were interested in playing nurse—"

"I was serious."

He arched an eyebrow. "So was I."

An exasperated sigh escaped her. "You wouldn't try to use the sob story of your poor brother to get in my pants, would you?"

"Sure." He shrugged. "Craig's a guy, he'd understand."

And to think, for a minute she'd been feeling…well, she wasn't sure what, but she hadn't wanted to smack him upside the head. That in itself was a big improvement over their exchanges in the office. He'd been completely obnoxious for the last couple of days, though admittedly in a playful way. She actually would have preferred a more intense attitude of straightforward competition, something that signaled he at least considered her a worthy adversary to be taken seriously. Something that didn't include wicked grins or boyish dimples.

"Mr. Brannon?" The question was from Elias Weaver, who stood behind his wife, Janice, as she moved through the doorway separating the waiting room from the treatment areas. "Didn't realize you'd joined us."

Hugh stood. "Just keeping Jocelyn company. And I wanted to convey Mr. Kimmerman's very sincere—"

"I'm not interested in anything Kimmerman has to say," Janice interrupted, her already brusque nature not exactly softened by the gravelly rasp in her voice. "I don't know why I kept considering you people this long, just hoping you'd come up with something that would justify the time I'd invested, I guess. We'll be signing with the Glengarry Group....as soon as I'm feeling well enough to meet with them."

Elias punctuated his wife's decision with a haughty sniff of disapproval, then helped her to the door.

Joss rubbed her hands across her face. "So much for that account."

"Cheer up, there's your meeting with Stanley next week. Just don't take him to the Salmonella Café."

Her jaw clenched.

"It was a joke, Joss."

"I'm sure this is very funny from your perspective." She marched toward the door, wanting to get home to a long, hot bubble bath. Make good use of that water heater she'd paid a fortune for earlier this week. She had to do something to improve her state of mind, and haunted as she was now by butterpecan reminiscences, she didn't think she could enjoy the bowl—oh, all right—carton of ice cream she'd promised herself.

Hugh followed after her. "You're too tense."

She rolled her eyes heavenward. "That's because I happen to be in a bad mood right now. I also happen to be entitled."

How could he understand the way she was feeling, she wondered, stepping outside and shivering slightly at the damp promise of rain in the cool night air. Hugh never failed. He was the boy at the front of the class who made As whether he cracked a book or not, the boy the rest of the students wanted to hate because he'd blown the curve for everyone else. Granted, Joss had made her share of As, but only after hours and hours of study. Then there'd been the time in college when she'd stayed up so late striving for perfection that she'd slept through the exam. *Irony, the fabric of my life.*

But despite his success, not even her best one hundred and ten percent effort would have enabled her to hate him.

"Things like this just don't happen to you," she muttered.

"And that's supposed to be my fault? *Most* people don't meet for business over ptomaine appetizers. You must be special."

She shot him an impatient excuse-me-but-I-believe-that's-my-last-nerve-you're-standing-on glare.

They were almost to her car, and she quickened her steps, eager to have this evening behind her. While it was true he hadn't managed to sign Weaver Investing, he hadn't sickened and alienated them, either. His efforts had kept Kimmerman in the running, and though Janice had said tonight she should've signed elsewhere before now, Joss's money would have been on Hugh to eventually wear the imperious woman down.

As she unlocked her car door, Joss sighed, torn between exasperation and reluctant gratitude for his company tonight. "Thanks. Showing up the way you did was decent."

"Don't sound so surprised. I can be a good guy."

He could be a lot of things.

She glanced up, suddenly realizing how close he stood. She'd missed his height, those broad shoulders, the feeling that he could wrap her in his arms and make her forget everything outside his embrace.

Despite his earlier flirtatious teasing with her, Hugh hadn't had any plans of trying to seduce Joss. The lady was high maintenance. She wanted perfection from herself and others, and could be as relaxing as gridlock traffic. But with the way she was staring up at him, her lips slightly parted, the flush in her cheeks unmistakable even in the jaundiced glow of the parking-lot lights, Hugh very much wanted to kiss her.

He brought his hands to her shoulders as he lowered his head. The kiss was an unlikely reunion—he hadn't expected to ever have Joss McBride in his arms again, and he was a little surprised she hadn't reacted in a way that left him needing the services of the E.R. behind him. Instead, she kissed him back, the shape and taste and movement of her every bit as sexy as he remembered.

There was no awkwardness, only a hungry familiarity, a relief to be kissing her again, his body asking why the hell it had been so long since he had.

But as she pulled away with a small gasp, it became very clear. Oh, yeah—Joss hadn't wanted him to kiss her anymore.

That must've slipped his mind.

He cut off any words of outrage she might have for him. "Guess I should've gone with the comforting hug instead?"

She swallowed. "I was thinking about sticking to handshakes from here on out."

They could try, but he was pretty sure even that would tempt him to touch her more. Besides, it presented an irresistible element of challenge...one he should really do his best to ignore.

Without glancing up at him, she opened her car door. "Good night, Hugh."

"See you tomorrow."

Having Joss in the office was a guilty pleasure. In addition to her being a wonderful asset to the company and exceedingly easy on the eyes, he genuinely liked her when she wasn't being stiff and uptight. And when she *was* in one of her competitive I-take-myself-so-seriously moods, it was fun to mess with her. Admittedly, his favorite times were when his wisecracks provoked her to retaliate. The lady had a wicked sense of humor, but he sometimes worried about it rusting with disuse.

As she backed her car up, he turned to find his own in the shining metallic rows of visitor parking. In his inexplicably dazed state, it took a second to recall what his vehicle even looked like.

She was so damn sexy.

And, unfortunately, so on edge. When he'd walked into that emergency room earlier, the waves of tension rolling off of her had been high enough he'd wondered if he'd need a surfboard to get near her. He knew she was upset about what had happened tonight, but blaming herself was just plain egocentric. Did she honestly believe there was any way she could have foreseen the fiasco? She'd had a well-prepared presentation and taken the client to a four-star restaurant. Tonight wasn't a failure on her part.

It was simply one of those things that happened…to other people.

Hugh started his own car, turning on the windshield wipers as a light drizzle began to fall. Try as he might, he couldn't think of a time he'd ever experienced one of life's unexpected little misfortunes. The closest he'd ever come was Craig's heart attack, but that had really been more unfortunate for *Craig*. His other brother Mitch had once teased that Hugh was the only person he knew who had a shot at ever experiencing one of those *Penthouse*-style scenarios that were too ridiculously good to be true—*and the pizza delivery girl just happened to be a gorgeous blonde doing her dissertation on the Kama Sutra….*

In fact, Hugh's older brother had remarked on Hugh's luck, too, but with more resentment than humor.

Not all of his success came from luck. *I have skills.* But luck and skill combined hadn't been enough to make things work with Joss.

7

SHORTLY BEFORE EIGHT O'CLOCK Thursday morning, Joss walked into the coffee room at Kimmerman's, needing a soda that would offer the stay-awake advantages of being both caffeinated and ice-cold. When she'd arrived home last night, she'd been too frustrated—emotionally and sexually—to go to bed. Her relaxing bath had left her more pruny than serene, so she'd gone to work painting in the dining room.

Beneath the chair rails she'd temporarily removed, she planned to paper the lower halves of the walls, but she was painting the top halves a gleaming ivory. The room, an old-fashioned formal dining area with a vaulted ceiling and chandelier, would be gorgeous when she was done with it. By the time she'd finished two of the walls, she'd been exhausted, but it was so refreshing to see her work visibly pay off that she hadn't wanted to stop.

Besides, she wouldn't be able to sleep with the job half finished. It would just eat at her…much like the memory of kissing Hugh.

"Hey, Joss." Nick stood at one of the vending machines, waiting for his healthy breakfast of mini-chocolate-chip cookies to drop. Unlike the glimpses she'd caught of him earlier in the week, he was dressed normally today in chinos and a sweater. Thank goodness he'd decided to just be himself.

"Morning. Nice to bump into you." They'd both been so busy with the transition that they hadn't had much of a chance to talk. But the times she'd seen him, he'd been collaborating with others in his department and seemed happy as a clam. Joss wondered idly what made clams happier than other mollusks.

Evil seafood and their wicked glee over ruining her career.

Nick squinted at her. "You feeling okay? 'Cause, no offense, but you're looking a little McBride of Frankenstein today."

Nothing like the honesty of friends. With her fair complexion, it would have taken a garish amount of makeup to conceal the dark circles under her eyes.

"Rough night," she admitted, pulling her wallet out of her purse and grabbing a couple of quarters. "I'm sure you'll hear the details later, but basically, my business dinner didn't go so well. We lost the client to the Glengarry Group."

"Ouch." Nick winced. "Guess you didn't need this so soon after not signing those people in Detroit. You aren't worried about losing your touch, are you?"

She gave him a wry grin. "Just for future reference, you have no career as a motivational speaker."

"Sorry. All I meant was that two strikes is nothing in the face of your batting average. You still get another chance to hit a homer."

"Sports metaphors? That's new."

He glanced downward, his smile shy. "I asked around about Lydia, and she likes, you know, manly men. Jocks."

"Lydia, the receptionist?" Joss recalled her first day, Lydia's tone of voice when she'd deemed Nick cute and asked if he was available. "I don't think you need sports know-how to impress her."

"Couldn't hurt, though, right?"

"I don't know. Being yourself might—"

"Joss, we're in advertising. You know how important image is." He popped a miniature cookie into his mouth. "See you at the meeting later?"

She nodded absently. Kimmerman was gathering people on both the business and creative sides to discuss what different clients wanted and what the copywriters and artists could reasonably do to meet those demands within budget. The account execs were liaisons between the firm and customer, and tried, sometimes in vain, to keep everyone happy. She thought there would also be some media buyers at the meeting today. And Kimmerman would probably mention again the "employee appreciation" day he'd set up at his country club for this weekend.

Attendance was not optional.

Armed with her caffeinated cola, Joss headed back toward her area of the building. She'd wanted to stop for the soda first, so she could dive straight into her work when she got inside her office. Now she realized she should have dropped off her purse first and asked if she could bring something back from the machines for Annette. Joss was determined to win the woman over. In a perhaps overzealous attempt to do just that, Joss had suggested yesterday an improvement to Annette's filing system that would make it easier for the woman to cross-reference client information. To say the helpful ideas had not been well-received would be an understatement.

Oh, well. Even if Joss had missed an opportunity to bring the woman a beverage, there was still good old-fashioned friendliness. "Morning, Annette."

The woman's lips thinned. It was hard to say if her expression was supposed to be a smile or a sneer. "Miss McBride. We wondered if you were coming in this morning."

Joss raised her eyebrows. She was what, two and a half minutes late? Annette and Vivian would really hit it off. "It's just now eight o'clock."

The receptionist's penciled eyebrows lifted. "I guess you're right. Mr. Brannon's been here so long I'd forgotten how early it was. But I thought maybe you'd take the morning off after your unfortunate incident last night. Heard your meeting with the Weavers put you in the hospital."

Actually, it had put *them* there, but that didn't sound any better than Annette's interpretation. Joss proceeded to her office without comment. Screw old-fashioned friendliness.

Had Hugh really been here all that long, or was mentioning his early arrival just another way for Annette to take a jab at Joss?

The last few days he'd shown up on time, maybe with a few minutes to spare, but certainly not markedly early. She knew because *she* routinely got to work markedly early. It was not a petty attempt to beat Hugh in some unspoken competition. She'd done the same when she'd worked for Wyatt...the Aruba-bound traitor.

Her morning was busy enough that she was able

to put aside thoughts of last night, except of course
when someone heckled her good-naturedly about
it. She'd expected Hugh to be the worst of the
offenders, but she barely saw him. While he could
normally be spotted at least a couple of times out on
the main floor, kidding around and brainstorming
with co-workers, today he seemed content to stay
closeted in his office. At least, that was the impression she received whenever she dared to venture
outside her own.

She knew that no one—besides Annette—meant
anything insulting by bringing up her disappointment with the Weavers. In fact, some people were
sympathetic or even downright congratulatory, since
few had relished the prospect of trying to keep Janice
Weaver happy. But even the most well-intended
comments did nothing but bring Joss back to the fact
that she hadn't won the account. So she kept herself
busy and isolated until it was time to meet in the
large conference room, where lunch was being
catered.

After stopping at the side table long enough to
pour a glass of water and spear a few pieces of fruit
onto a paper plate, Joss squeezed in at the expansive
oak conference table beside Nick. Kimmerman Jr.
was already seated at one end, between the produc-
tion manager and creative director, but his father had
yet to arrive, so people were mostly munching on the
provided goodies and gossiping.

Nick was telling Joss about having input on his
first commercial when Hugh walked in. She tried to
stay focused on what her friend was saying, but it
was hard to concentrate when all her hormones had

suddenly gone to a DefCon Four state of alertness. She cast a covert sidelong glance in Hugh's direction.

He was wearing a deep green shirt tucked in black slacks, and the crisp businesslike image was softened only by the way his cuffs were rolled up and his hair was spiky in a couple of places where he might've been running his hands through it. She experienced an involuntary memory of running her own fingers through the silky strands and swallowed a sigh. His hair was so thick that one might expect it to be more coarse than soft, but—

Nick elbowed her in the ribs, but before she could get out the appropriate "ouch, dammit," she realized that someone was speaking to her.

"Jocelyn?"

She blinked, turning to find Robert Kimmerman peering at her in concern. "Sir?"

"I just wanted to tell you that I'm sure your presentation last night would have been top-notch, had that unforeseen fiasco not occurred. Wyatt Allen sang your praises, as have many individuals you've worked with."

"Th-thank you." She tried to smile at his words of support, but inside she was mortified. The president of the company had been speaking to her, and she'd been too preoccupied with Hugh Brannon's *hair* to notice? Good to know her priorities weren't completely whacked or anything.

Since Kimmerman believed in efficiency and wisely realized this meeting took them all away from the jobs he paid them to do, he kept the conversation moving at a brisk enough pace to prohibit Joss from dwelling on anything ridiculous like, say, someone's scalp or follicles. Kimmerman also reminded them of the "picnic" on Saturday, though she doubted the country-club gathering would be of the casual blankets-on-the-ground, here-come-the-ants variety.

"And I have some good news," he said, leaning forward to prop his chin on his steepled fingers. "The chairman of Lynwood Fitness Equipment, manufacturers of some very popular home-gym equipment and suppliers to numerous gyms around the country, recently had a direct-mail disaster. When he looked into it, Colin Lynwood discovered that the agency they've been paying an exorbitant amount to has been freelancing the jobs out to an assortment of small organizations. Lynwood isn't happy with the inconsistent results and the lack of personal attention. He's leaked it that he's willing to consider other firms. I'm thinking of assigning someone to him, to sound him out and see if it would be worth our while to do a speculative campaign."

Joss broke into a wide smile, perhaps her first genuinely happy one of the day. Could it be she'd just been handed the opportunity for the home run Nick had predicted that morning? *Thank you, fate.* "Mr. Kimmerman, if I may say something…?"

The stately man nodded. "By all means."

"It might be worth mentioning that Visions was in the running for the HardBodies 2000 account earlier this year. When I was working on that, I did a lot of research in the field, including a study of their major competitor, Lynwood." There were a lot more account execs here than there'd been at Visions, and the data she'd compiled could be invaluable in earning her a chance to be the rep for the fitness manufacturer.

Kimmerman sat back in his chair, looking impressed. "Then it seems we have a double advantage."

"Double?" Joss echoed, a pang of irrational wariness disturbing her newfound affection for fate.

Her answer didn't come from the company president, but from farther down the table. Specifically, from Hugh Brannon. "I went to college with Lynwood's brand manager."

With a sinking heart, she craned her head around Nick and met Hugh's bright blue eyes, feeling an unwanted pull of attraction even as she wanted to throw an eraser at him for having the devil's own luck. The man was a statistical anomaly. "College?"

"UT. Class of '94." He grinned, making a sign with his index finger and pinky and waving at her. "Hook 'em horns."

Fate, you bitch.

"I'M SORRY," EMILY SAID, a muffled snort escaping. "I don't mean to laugh, it's just—"

"The woman was seriously ill." Joss gave her friend a stern look. "Trust me, it wasn't funny."

"I know," Emily agreed. And then dissolved into giggles.

Deciding to take the dignified approach and ignore Em, Joss steered the shopping cart toward the line of registers at the front of the do-it-yourself store. She'd left work early today on a research trip to help prepare for her meeting with Stanley Patone. The fact that it got her out of the office was simply a bonus. If her morning of people commenting on the Weavers had been uncomfortable, it was nothing compared to her mounting tension this afternoon as

Kimmerman deliberated over which of his execs to send after Lynwood Fitness Equipment. Why did so many things seem to come down to a standoff between her and Hugh, and why did her track record against him seem so inadequate? That inner voice she'd grown accustomed to insisted she must not be trying hard enough.

Since Emily didn't have classes on Thursday afternoon, she'd met Joss to lend a sympathetic ear—when she wasn't collapsing into gales of hilarity—and an opinion on paint samples for the master bedroom. The room desperately needed to be recarpeted, too, but Joss had yet to determine the perfect color scheme.

As they passed a display of caulking guns, she noticed a tall bearded man watching Emily appreciatively. Joss would've pointed out his obvious interest if she'd thought it would help boost her friend's self-esteem, but judging from his scraggly shoulder-length hair and the lewd slogan on his black T-shirt, Em would see him as further evidence that she didn't attract the right sort of guy.

"Hey," Joss said suddenly, embarrassed by her memory lapse, "did I tell you I met someone you might like?" Some best friend she was, having forgotten about that until now. Maybe if she spent less time thinking about H—the house.

Emily raised her eyebrows. "At work?"

"No, in the neighborhood. He lives one street over from me, got some of my mail by mistake, and I was just driving up when he brought it by. Single, attractive, civil engineer. And he didn't mention a fondness for pretentious foreign films."

"That's a good start…but if he's so single and attractive, are you sure you don't have any interest in him? You did see him first."

In the ten minutes she'd conversed with Paul, it hadn't occurred to Joss to consider him as a potential date for herself. He'd been pleasant and funny, with a kind face and wide brown eyes. But there'd definitely been no little thrill of attraction. Nothing like the zing she'd felt when Hugh massaged the base of her neck last night, or the melting liquid sensation she'd felt when he'd kissed her.

"I've got my hands too full with the house and the new job to think about my own love life."

Emily studied her for a long moment before nodding. "Fair enough. But, um…I might actually have met someone I'd like to get to know better, too."

Joss brightened. "Really?"

"I would've said something sooner, but you had so much interesting news. Besides, I don't know that anything will come out of it, I hardly know him. He's a research librarian at the university."

Hmm. If he was quiet and gentle, he could be great for Em, but shy introverted librarians were a stereotype. Besides, he could be scholarly and just as intellectually arrogant as Simon. "Have you guys talked?"

"Sort of. Our longest conversation to date was about the *Chicago Manual of Style*. Not exactly scintillating, but he's cute."

"Then go for it. Maybe next time you go to the library, you can ask for his help finding some risqué research materials." Joss waggled her eyebrows. "Seduce him in the stacks."

"Right." Emily laughed. "This from a woman who probably clocked forty hours a week studying in the library when she was in college."

"The *wrong* college, apparently," Joss muttered.

"Do you think Kimmerman is going to put Hugh on the account?"

"Well, he is great at his job, and he does already have a bond with these people." Plus, he had the sexiest eyes she'd ever seen, but that probably would've been more helpful if the brand manager was female. And what was Joss doing thinking about his eyes, anyway?

They got in line behind a man buying some sort of table saw, and Joss cast a guilty sidelong glance at Emily, as though her friend might somehow discern that Joss was thinking about Hugh in nonprofessional ways. In relaying the story of last night's events, Joss had neglected to mention only one thing—Hugh's kissing her. But she'd regained her senses and moved away from him so quickly it hardly counted.

Her body warmed at the memory, and she reflexively licked her lips. *Oh, it counted.*

All right, yes, Hugh was a great kisser. He was great at a lot of things...including sapping her concentration and her self-confidence. What she needed for her bedroom right now was a color scheme, not a man.

8

"CAN YOU BELIEVE THIS?" Joss demanded as she squirted toothpaste onto the brush. "Saturday! My day to sleep in, and I have to go to this work thing."

From between the parted curtains in the bathroom window, Dulcie leveled her owner a sardonic blue-eyed look. One that said, "Since when do you sleep in?"

The cat had a point. But still, Joss should be here to oversee the contractor who was finishing the deck today—she'd believe it when she saw it—and replacing some of the floorboards in the second story of the house, ensuring that Joss wouldn't find herself one day suddenly on the first story. *And* she had a dining room to finish and work she'd brought home with her!

Although maybe it was good she was getting out—she knew her presentation for Stanley Patone by heart and if she stayed home she'd be too tempted to work on a pitch for Lynwood that would probably turn out to be a waste of time.

A slight stinging in her gums alerted her to the fact that she was perhaps brushing a tad too hard, and she rinsed, trying to decide what to wear. It was too cool for swimming, but the Indian-summer warmth of the last few days would make it plenty comfortable for people to use the tennis courts or golf course Kimmerman had told them about. The morning was devoted to "team-building" exercises, then they'd eat and socialize until such time as they thought they could sneak away without incurring their employer's wrath.

She changed into a black tennis skort and blue-and-black top. She'd just finished braiding her blond hair when the contractor arrived.

Forty-five minutes later, she drove into the private parking lot of the Riverbrook—wasn't that just a *tad* redundant?—Club. Once her car had been turned over to valet service, she walked inside the clubhouse, where a sign reading Welcome Kimmerman and Kimmerman sat in the lobby. Richly upholstered armchairs were arranged on expensive area rugs, and vases of fresh flowers filled the room. Joss imagined that on cooler days, the two available fireplaces were quite cozy.

Following the sign's directions, she turned to the stairs on her left that led down into a private hall. About a half-dozen of her co-workers had arrived, and they milled around in expensive casual wear, chatting amiably. Joss was delighted to see Cherie Adams, the plump brunette receptionist from Visions, who had been wrapping things up at that office for the past week.

Joss hugged the older woman. "You have no idea how much I missed you!" Whereas Cherie had always been a breath of fresh air, Annette was like a lungful of exhaust fumes. "When do you move over to the office?"

"A week from Monday. And that Mr. Kimmerman's real nice, he's come by a couple of times to assure me I'm an important part of the team."

Joss nodded. It still chafed that the company she'd been trying to help Wyatt build had been swallowed up by an agency higher on the food chain, but she had to admit, she had a good employer. At least Kimmerman showed no immediate signs of retiring or being indicted.

"Have you seen Nick?" Joss asked.

Cherie shook her head. "Not yet. Alicia Kennedy's in the corner, though, and I was just about to go say hi to her. I'll catch up with you later!"

Joss waggled her fingers in goodbye before turning to scan the room again.

Her gaze collided with Hugh Brannon's as he came down the stairs and ducked into the room.

Although Hugh had known he'd see Joss today, he hadn't expected her to be wearing a little black skirt that made the most of her smooth muscular legs. He stopped short at the bottom of the stairs, drinking in the sight of her. A moment passed and he realized dimly that he'd crossed the line between an admiring glance and staring. He should really stop—and he would. An-n-ny minute now.

It wasn't that Joss's sporty skirt was shorter than what some of the other ladies were wearing, it was just that he had vivid recollections of those particular legs being wrapped around him. He averted his eyes. He might not be able to erase the image in his head—why would any red-blooded male want to?—but he could at least avoid a sexual harassment suit.

Another man called out Joss's name, and she

turned, smiling. It suddenly occurred to Hugh that she might actually have brought a *date* to this thing; Kimmerman had said guests and family were welcome to participate in lunch and the afternoon activities. Hugh was reassured to see she was only talking to that kid from visuals…Nick something. The undeniable relief Hugh felt was alarming. Did he care that much about his ex-girlfriend's social life?

He should have asked Kristine to come with him. She might have enjoyed the club's facilities—he knew she loved racquetball and golf. If it was too cold to use the pools, that still left the hot tubs…yet the only woman he could imagine sliding into the steamy velvety water with was Jocelyn.

Never one for denying himself what he wanted, he walked toward her. When she glanced up, he would have bet everything in his 401 that the glimmer he saw in her jade eyes was answering heat.

"Joss. You look nice."

She shifted her weight, as if uncomfortable with the simple compliment. "Thanks. You, um…you, too."

He was wearing a pair of khaki shorts with a golf shirt, nothing special. But they both knew she liked what she saw, and he had a mad urge to ask how she felt about blowing off the team-building exercises and finding the hot tub. Neither of them took much notice as Nick excused himself.

"So, what approach did you have in mind?" she blurted suddenly.

Well, there was always candles and wine…trite, but effective. Talking dirty was an option if—

"With Lynwood Fitness," she added. "Because I was thinking—"

"About business." He sighed heavily. "You're always thinking about business."

"Not always. I have very well-rounded interests. It's just that some of us need the extra focus if we're going to succeed." She glanced at the floor for a moment. "I guess we all can't have your luck."

Anger scratched at him. She knew better than anyone, from their work together at Mitman, that he busted his ass to get the job done and get it done right. On Thursday and Friday, he'd actually arrived at the office before Joss did, and he'd tuned out the action blockbuster on television last night to devote his thoughts to the Lynwood campaign, should Kimmerman decide to make use of Hugh's connections rather than Joss's research.

"Winners make their own luck, Joss. Losers make excuses." Perhaps not the best thing to say to someone with Joss's competitive drive, but dammit, he'd landed plenty of accounts with people he *hadn't* known in college. He'd won awards.

"You know what, Hugh? You're right." She gave him an acidic smile. "And I'm certainly not making myself any luck standing here."

She pivoted and stalked off. Her tone might've been bitter, but the woman had one sweet backside. He supposed he could kiss the hot-tub fantasies goodbye.

Annoyed as he was, he couldn't stifle the attraction that had been there from the day they'd met. In the bedroom, they always got along. Outside of that, she drove him crazy.

Take today, for instance, and how quick she was to write off his talent, crediting his successes to luck, agency resources or deals with the devil. He wanted her respect. The realization surprised him, but why *shouldn't* he have her respect?

Joss was wrong about him, and it suddenly seemed important to prove that. She needed a new perspective, and he was just the man to give it to her.

Joss WAS SITTING in a white lawn chair on the spacious wooden deck, pushing potato salad around her plate with a plastic fork, when Nick approached her, his steps tentative.

"Anybody sitting there?" He gestured to an empty chair with the iced tea in his hand.

"Nope. But I'm surprised you didn't try to get a seat near Lydia."

Nick frowned. "Some copywriter beat me to it. Besides, I thought it might look better for you if I joined you."

"Look better?" She angled her head and gave him a puzzled smile. "I was just taking a break from the hectic activity of this morning. Do I seem pathetic over here by myself?"

He scooted his chair in closer to the round glass-topped table. "No, you seem antisocial. You know how intent Kimmerman is on making us feel like one big happy family."

She realized that Nick sounded awfully serious, as if he really was concerned she was failing their boss. Great.

"I participated like crazy this morning," she reminded him. "Heck, he made me one of the team captains."

Nick stared at her for a second, then stuffed a fork-

ful of food in his mouth as though that would save
him from answering.

"Nick?"

He swallowed. "Well…I'm not sure he meant for
the obstacles to be approached as, you know, a blood
sport."

Reflecting back on the morning, she thought she'd
been pretty successful at getting her team to work
well together—with the exception of Annette, whom
Joss would have suspected of attempted sabotage,
were she the paranoid type. Everyone had seemed to
have fun. Especially when she—they—had beat
Hugh's team.

Why wasn't Nick chastising Hugh, the other team
captain? The man had approached the games with
the same intensity. For a change, though, he'd lost, so
why wasn't she feeling more ebullient?

She and Nick ate in companionable silence, until
she happened to glance up and see Lydia Jenkins ap-
proaching. Under the table, Joss subtly nudged Nick
with her foot.

"Don't look now," she said ventriloquist-style,
"but I think someone's headed your way."

He immediately whipped his head around to spot
Lydia, then glanced back at Joss, his expression nervous and his skin blotchy. "What do I do?"

"Saying hello might be a start," she said encouragingly. "Guess that copywriter just wasn't her type."

Bolstered, he looked up with a shaky grin. "Hi,
Lydia."

"Hi, Nick." The petite redhead smiled. "I'm not interrupting, am I?"

"Not at all," Joss said. "Nick was just being kind

enough to keep me company. Would you like to have a seat?"

The receptionist shook her head. "That's okay. I have to go help Kimmerman with the awards he's handing out for fun, recognizing people's achievements from this morning, giving the a-chain-is-only-as-strong speech. But, Nick, I wanted to ask you...I know how you're into sports and all—"

Joss choked on her lemonade, but thankfully no one paid any attention. The only sports she knew him to play regularly were of the video-game variety.

"—and I wondered if you'd like to check out the tennis courts after lunch. Hugh Brannon and I were talking about playing, and I thought you might be interested in some mixed doubles...?"

Nick did his best impression of a deer caught in a pair of high beams. "I, uh—Joss, wanna be on my team?"

Lydia's eyebrows shot up, and Joss got the impression the younger woman had been hoping Nick would partner with *her.* But maybe he was hoping Joss could make him look good in the eyes of the pretty receptionist.

"Sure." The opportunity to beat Hugh again was irresistible. "Sounds like fun."

ONCE THE COIN HAD BEEN TOSSED to decide which team would serve first, Joss and Nick walked toward their side of the court.

"Tell me you know *something* about this game," Joss whispered under her breath.

He nodded. "I get the rules. I've watched matches on TV."

That was a start. They certainly didn't have time for the intricacies of tennis right now. "Ever played?"

"Ping-pong. That's pretty close, right?"

Her eye twitched. "I'll serve first."

Predictably, Hugh took the ad side, leaving Lydia the deuce. Joss hit a strong, but not tricky, serve over the net, warming up and testing the other woman's skill. The receptionist easily returned the ball. Nick—holding his racket like a baseball bat—swung, dropping his racket in the process.

All righty. Joss obviously needed to give the game everything she had if she didn't want the quickest love-six set in club history.

Her next serve was to Hugh, and when she glanced across the net at his smug smile, irritation radiated through her body and into her racket as if it were an extension of her arm. She aimed for the lines of the service box, but emotion clouded her concentration. She faulted.

Hugh smirked. "So, the tennis skirt is just decorative, then?"

She ignored the trash talk and took her second serve. *Ace.* Hot damn.

Despite the fact that she had to carry her team, Joss and Nick managed to win a couple of games. Exhilaration added a bounce to her step.

As the two teams switched sides, Hugh passed her, his confident grin wolfish. "You're going down, McBride."

"You wish, Brannon."

But Joss and Nick were clearly outmatched, and the first set went to Hugh and his partner, six-three. During the second set, however, Nick finally managed to hit his stride—and the ball, wonder of wonders. His serves needed work, but when they weren't on the side of the court facing the sun, he did okay. Once the ball was in play, Joss covered the entire court. At four-all, she began to feel they really had a chance at this set, putting them in contention for the match.

Granted, this wasn't exactly the U.S. Open, but as she dashed across the hard-court surface, artfully whacking the hell out of the fuzzy yellow ball, it seemed that all the frustration she'd felt with her job, with her house, with men...everything dissolved except for her intense focus and desire to win.

Hugh served the ball and surprisingly, it went out.

Joss raised her eyebrows. "Sun in your eyes? Oh, wait. *We're* facing the sun."

His next serve was good, and his team got the point when Nick went after a ball she could have easily returned. Apparently, her teammate had grown cocky after a few good hits and wanted to show off for Lydia.

Five-four. If Hugh's team picked up this last point, he and Lydia would be best two out of three. Joss would lose. She wasn't going to let that happen.

She zeroed in on the ball, willing it to her racket, determined to outplay her opponents, determined to—

Smash. Her partner collided with her, knocking her down. It occurred to her as she fell that her foot really shouldn't bend in quite that direction, but it took another moment for her mind to register the throbbing pain in her ankle.

Nick dropped down beside her. "I'm so sorry. I tried to stop. Didn't you hear me call it?"

She hadn't heard anything but the voice in her head telling her to get the shot. To win.

Hugh vaulted over to her side of the court. "Can you wiggle your toes? Can you stand up?"

"Of course I can stand." But when she attempted to do just that, fire shot through her left ankle. "On one foot, anyway."

Nick was supporting her weight, but Hugh relieved the younger man of the task by lifting Joss into his arms.

Cologne wafted over her, mixed with the smell of the autumn day and the sweat he'd worked up during their tennis match. His muscled arms tightened around her body, and Joss suddenly had a better understanding of her cat. Despite the discomfort in her ankle, she had to fight the urge to purr or rub herself against Hugh's warm body.

Once they'd removed her shoe and sock and seen the purple swollen ankle, he carried her toward the clubhouse. He whistled under his breath as he walked, and if she didn't know better, she'd think Hugh kind of liked carting her around in her annoyingly dependent state. There had been a time when she'd been tempted to lean on Hugh, but even as she'd realized her feelings for him were deepening, he'd seemed to see their relationship as some type of game. How could she have a real connection with someone she couldn't share her victories with? Since they'd worked together at Mitman, his response to her triumphs had seemed to be an energized, "Just you wait, I'll win next time." And trying to share her failures, which she wasn't really built for anyway, had been even worse. The one time she'd been really upset, when a client had mocked her ideas in front of her employer, Hugh had swooped in and won the account she'd been killing herself to try to get.

She was almost grateful for the physical ache in her ankle to take her mind off a time when she'd forgotten to depend on herself. The on-staff medic poked at the tender flesh and pronounced Joss should get X rays, just to be on the safe side—and, of course, to keep the club clear of any liability issues.

"I can drive you," Hugh volunteered

Wouldn't be my first choice. Cherie had gone home, though. And Hugh had encouraged Nick and Lydia to check out the club's hot tub, insisting there was no reason all of them should wait with Joss, despite the other man's guilt-stricken protests.

"All right," she agreed grudgingly.

"I'll get you home, then take a cab from your place. Hold on just a second, and let me find someone who can drop my car off for me."

Like she was going anywhere?

Hugh returned moments later, once again whistling in annoyingly high spirits. "All set. Let's get you to the emergency room."

Oh, good. Because she definitely hadn't spent enough time *there* this week.

9

AFTER JOSS AND her badly sprained ankle had finally been released from the E.R., Hugh helped her into the back of his car. The doctor had given her something for the pain, and after jotting down some directions, Joss slept a little. It was dark, and Hugh's stomach growled with the realization that they'd missed dinner.

He'd sat in that tacky waiting room for what felt like hours—probably because it had been hours—more than enough time to get him thinking about Craig again, recalling how the family had huddled in the waiting room, wanting news and hating the collective feeling of helplessness. Hadn't Hugh decided then that life was too short to stress yourself out over every little thing? What had he been trying to prove on the tennis court today? It should've been a stupid throwaway game between co-workers after lunch, yet by the time they'd reached that last serve, he'd been hungry not just to win, but to decimate his opponent.

And bravo to you, pal. Now she's got an ankle brace and a prescription for painkillers.

He didn't feel responsible for Joss's fall, he just wasn't sure why he'd let himself walk around all day with a chip on his shoulder. She brought out a side of him he didn't much like. He'd thought to himself earlier that she needed a new outlook, which was true, but she didn't need to take Hugh more seriously and respect him more. She needed to take herself *less* seriously and have more fun with life.

He had to be careful not to get sucked into the same intensity she exuded. Maybe he should keep more distance between them. A smarter man would call Kristine, have a nice casual no-one-ends-up-in-the-E.R. time.

Hugh glanced in his rearview mirror, catching the barest glimpse of Joss sprawled on the back seat, her breathing soft and even, her skirt riding up in a tantalizing way no gentleman—good thing he wasn't one of those—would ogle. With that single glance, he confirmed what he'd been fearing since he'd kissed Joss the other day—his convenient, no-explanations-needed, if-we're-both-still-free association with Kristine was over. Being with her would feel too much like settling for vanilla ice cream just because there was some in the house, when what he *really* wanted was butter pecan.

He turned off of the main road onto a smaller, curvy street that led him by some ritzy subdivisions. If Joss was living in one of these, she'd been making more money at Visions than he'd realized. But her directions led him past those first neighborhoods, into an area populated with smaller brand-new homes. He could easily picture her in one, surrounded by pale wall-to-wall carpet and sleek silver kitchen appliances, maybe with one of those flat-top ranges.

When he didn't see the street name she'd written down, he began to think he'd missed it in the dark.

"Joss," he said over his shoulder. "I need you to wake up, honey."

"Mmm. Okay," she murmured drowsily, before resuming the exact same breathing pattern.

He tried again, a bit louder. "Joss?"

She started, and he saw her sit up in the back seat, rubbing her eyes. "Hey."

"Sorry, Sleeping Beauty, but I can't shake this feeling that I passed your house several subdivisions ago."

Yawning, she looked out the window. "Nope. My street's coming up. Not the next left, but the one after."

"Oh. Okay." He drove farther away from the new neighborhoods with their community clubhouses and private pools.

When they got to the street she'd indicated, he turned, surprised by what he could make out in the lamplight. The sprawling neighborhood was older than he'd expected—dotted with ranch and two stories, both brick and vinyl-siding, with occasional stonework. The fences, if present at all, varied in style. Clearly, this was not a subdivision run by one of those homeowner's societies that voted on what sort of mailbox you could put up.

He'd envisioned her not just living under the rules of such a neighborhood government, but possibly running it.

"Interesting street," he remarked.

"*I* like it," she said, a defensive note in her voice.

He laughed. "So do I. I didn't mean interesting as in 'I can't think of something nice to say,' I just meant, it's not as shiny and boring as I'd anticipated."

"Gee. Thanks." She tapped on the glass. "That one, on the right. Just before the cul-de-sac."

As he pulled the car into a long driveway, he wished he could see more of the house Joss had chosen. It was a two story with a large porch and several impressive trees in the yard. He parked under the carport and turned off the ignition.

"Stay right there." He hopped out of the car. With most people who had sprained ankles, you wouldn't think it necessary to tell them to wait for assistance. But he wouldn't have put it past Joss to try to hobble into the house alone.

When he reached down for her, she drew back into the car's leather interior. "I don't really need to be carried. I can just lean on you." Even that was a grudging concession.

"Yeah, but it's not very well lit, and your body may be groggier than you realize from those painkillers." Why sacrifice this rare opportunity to hold her?

She sighed. "All right. Hang on a sec, let me get out my keys." Beneath the dome interior light of the car, she dug through her purse, retrieving her key ring with a metallic jangle.

Joss scooted her feet out of the car and leaned forward so that he could pick her up. She was all womanly softness against him, and his body reacted with very male hardness. *Oh, baby.*

"Why did we break up again?" he asked before he could stop himself.

She tilted her head back to stare him straight in the eye. "Might have had something to do with the way you screwed me out of an account. Or was it a rhetorical question?"

He carried her across a brick pathway to the front of the house. "Joss, we'd competed for accounts before, and it was always 'to the victor go the spoils.' I even seem to recall some very interesting bets." Wagers in which there were no real losers. What had been different with the stupid Stefan's Salons contract?

"Those were open competition. This felt... sneaky," she said quietly.

She had a minor point there, but it wasn't as if he'd been trying to hide his intent from her. The idea for the campaign had been a spontaneous one. Joss had repeatedly taken ideas to the prospective client, only to be turned down each time—once in front of some of Mitman's bigwigs. When Hugh had taken her to the Waif for a late dinner and sympathetic ear, she'd told him she could've just died when Stefan derided her pitch and the vice president had hastened to add his own displeasure, despite praising the campaign a day earlier.

At a meeting the next day, Hugh had shared a spur-of-the-moment concept—hair vigilantes, ads showing women who had wrongly taken styling matters into their own hands. The first had been titled "Couldn't you just dye?" His favorite had been a billboard featuring a member of the style police with a bullhorn, instructing a young woman to "step *away* from the home perm, ma'am."

Hugh walked up the creaky steps of the wooden porch. "Maybe you said something that gave me an idea, but it's not as if I took yours. Last we'd talked, you were fresh out of them."

"Exactly." Her soft, resigned sigh was muffled by the sounds of the breeze and tree frogs. "And you didn't even seem to care about how frustrating that was for me. I'd worked for hours, *days*, racking my brain to try to make this guy happy, which you knew. Then you waltz into that meeting, no warning before-hand, with some idea that just popped to mind, something you'd put zero time into, making me…"

He shifted his weight as she unlocked the door. If she'd somehow got the impression he didn't care, maybe it was just because she let herself care too much about things. "It was just one account, Joss. One meaningless loss in your very successful career."

"Meaningless! I—" She cut herself off and took a deep breath. "It's in the past. There's no point in our discussing this."

Probably not. He wasn't sure why he'd brought it up in the first place. He hadn't been looking for a fight.

He carried her inside, pausing as she reached past his shoulder to hit the foyer light switch. Her breasts pressed against him, and a light vanilla scent tickled his nose pleasantly. But the moment was short-lived. An overhead bulb illuminated the small entryway, and Joss recoiled from him as quickly as she could without toppling to the tile floor below.

Actually, it was sheet flooring, he realized. Patterned to look like tile, but cracked and stained in several places.

"Since we didn't crash through the porch," Joss said unexpectedly, "I'm hoping that means the con-tractor finished his work today, on schedule. Living room's in there."

On his right was a wall and a staircase, to his left a dark room that seemed huge. Joss was pointing straight ahead, and he carried her through a carpeted hallway that opened with a spacious kitchen on one side and the living room she'd mentioned on the other. On the opposite end of the room, the hallway picked up again, just long enough for a small room off to the left that he guessed was a bathroom. There was also a back door that led out into a yard too dark to see.

He recognized the couch from when he and Joss had been together, but everything else was something of a shock. She'd left a light on above the kitchen sink, putting the oddly mismatched room into clear view. The walls were a pretty pastel mural of blues and yellow—except for a patch of bright red between the sink and kitchen window. The fridge was an unattractive mustard-gold color and looked as though it should be part of a museum exhibit on the history of refrigeration. Then there was the gaping hole where he imagined a stove went.

She cleared her throat. "It's, um, under construction. If you could just get me to the sofa…"

"Good idea. You're not getting any lighter," he teased to cover his reluctance to set her down.

"Hey!"

He placed her on the couch, then flipped on the lamp that sat on her coffee table, taking another glance around. He couldn't reconcile the surroundings to the polished perfectionist he knew. It gave him hope.

"Well, thank you very much for everything," she said. "Have a nice night."

He raised his eyebrows and laughed. "'Don't let the door hit you in the ass' would have been more subtle, J."

"I—I just didn't want you to feel obligated to stay and help. I can take it from here."

"Never doubted it. But maybe I could impose for a few minutes, anyway? I'm starving, and there's no reason for you to putter around in the kitchen if you don't have to."

She bit her lip. "Now that you mention it, I could go for something to eat."

"I'd offer to fix us something, but I think someone stole your oven while you were out."

Her lips quirked into a half smile. "The Salvation Army picked up the stove yesterday. I donated it. The new one's due this week. Meantime, I've got the microwave. Best of all, it can actually be plugged into a kitchen outlet now."

He didn't want to know.

"Is there something you'd like me to nuke?" he asked instead.

"Why don't we just order a pizza? There's a place a few blocks away that doesn't take long. Things have been kind of crazy, and about the only thing I've managed to grab in the way of groceries is cat food.... Wait a sec." She'd been reclining lengthwise on the couch, leaning against the arm and propping her foot on a sofa pillow. Now she sat straight up, her body tensed.

"Joss? What's the matter?"

"Dulcie always comes to greet me when I get home. Well, less 'greets' and more guilts me for having the audacity to leave the house."

Dulcie? Ah, yes, the piranha with fur. The Siamese had never liked Hugh much, hissing at him whenever Joss's back was turned. For the most part, the cat seemed content to glare and bathe herself disdainfully, but there'd been occasions when Hugh and the cat had been "playing." Only he hadn't known it until she'd launched herself at him. His sole hope of ducking her guerilla attacks had been glancing in her direction in time to see the telltale butt-wiggle before she pounced.

"Dulcie?" Joss called out in a much sweeter voice than she'd ever used with Hugh. She glanced at him, gnawing on her bottom lip. "I hope the contractor didn't accidentally let her out. She's strictly an indoor cat, and this is still pretty unfamiliar territory to her."

"She's probably just holed up somewhere. Taking a catnap."

Joss rolled her eyes at the pun. "Would you do me a favor?"

Why hadn't he just left when she'd tried to kick him out in the first place? "Sure."

"Go to the bottom of the steps and call her, in case she's up in my room and didn't hear me?"

Heaving a sigh, he padded toward the foyer, whistling. "Dulcie! Here, cat." He clapped his hands together and whistled again for good measure.

"She's not a *dog*." Clearly doubting his ability to figure out how to summon a cat on his own, Joss crooned, "Dulcie." Then she made some kind of soft, coaxing sound with her lips.

Hugh peered around the door frame. "I'm not doing kissy noises."

Joss pushed herself up, using the arm of the sofa for balance. "I'll bet that contractor *did* let her out."

"Whoa, where do you think you're going?" he demanded. "If she's outside, I'll get her. You have a cordless phone?"

"Yeah." She paused. "It's up in my bedroom."

It was too far to tell from where he stood, but he thought she might've blushed a little. The couch was the same as before, he wondered if the bed was, too. Some good times had taken place on that particular piece of furniture.

"I thought I'd let you order the pizza while I go outside and try to find the little…Siamese."

Joss nodded. "It's the first door on the left at the top of the stairs. The phone's on my nightstand. Just don't walk under the ceiling fan, there's a weak floorboard that may or may not have been fixed today."

He took the stairs two at a time, shaking his head at her unexpected choice of houses. Light from her room spilled out onto the landing, coming from a delicate lamp with a pleated shade and curvy base. He wasn't surprised to see that Joss had made her bed neatly before leaving for the employee picnic that morning. Nothing hung on the walls yet, and the room was so tidy that it didn't begin to hint at the strong personality of the woman who lived here.

But then his gaze fell on the satiny peach robe hanging on a hook by her closet door, and his heart beat a little faster as he easily imagined her in the thin garment. Since it went without saying that he didn't want to be one of those weirdoes who ended up sniffing a woman's clothing or snooping around her personal belongings, he grabbed the phone and headed back down the steps so quickly it was a wonder he didn't trip and plow into the front door.

He strode into the living room, then tossed the phone onto the sofa cushion next to her. "Be right back."

Something was seriously wrong with his life, he

thought as he shut the front door behind him. He should be spending a Saturday night with a woman who laughed at his jokes and lusted after his body. Instead, he'd was standing out in the bushes making kissy noises for his ex-girlfriend's cat.

JOSS ORDERED an extra-large supreme, then closed her eyes, dissatisfied at sitting like a bump on a log, but a little relieved to be out of Hugh's company for a few minutes. The man had an affect on her that was far more debilitating than any sprain.

Though her hormones undeniably buzzed to life every time he touched her, it wasn't just her body that appreciated him. He'd been patient and funny this afternoon, relieving the excruciating boredom of waiting for the doctor to see her. And Joss had been completely unprepared for his wistful expression when he'd asked her why they'd split up. Did he miss her? His voice had held a certain yearning that she'd responded to against her will.

Until she'd remembered why they *had* split up.

During their brief relationship, she'd had to wrestle more than once with the feeling of being in his shadow, but she'd fallen in love with him, anyway. As far as she could tell, however, he hadn't returned the emotion. The crux of their relationship for him seemed to be the thrill of competition.

She didn't get the sense that he really knew her. If he did, he wouldn't be telling her now that the account he'd won had been "meaningless." He was right—it was just one account. But it had also been the one person she'd felt closest to kicking her while she was down. As a professional, she could've dealt with her lover succeeding where she had failed if he'd given any indication of understanding. What was more frustrating than watching him succeed with so little effort was the way he made light of her feelings. She couldn't entrust her heart to someone who could hurt her so easily without thinking anything of it.

They'd shared some good times, though. And it was hard to be aggravated with a man who hadn't eaten in hours and was out in the dark looking for a cat who'd never liked him. Maybe she should have limped as far as the front porch and sat there to call Dulcie—what were the odds the Siamese would come to Hugh anyway?

Joss knew she should stay off her ankle as much as possible tonight and tomorrow, but the doctor had said crutches wouldn't be necessary, as long as she didn't further injure herself. He'd told her to expect some soreness, but that the anti-inflammatories he'd prescribed would help with the swelling. By next week, she should be back to normal.

The front door closed with a bang, and Joss heard muttered curses, followed by hissing. Hugh rounded the corner into the living room, the cranky chocolate point cradled in his arms.

"Your cat, I believe." He carried Dulcie to her, but just as he leaned down to hand Joss the cat, the Siamese finally wriggled free and tore off down the hallway.

"Thank you." Joss smiled up at him, but then her eyes widened in chagrin. He had two shallow scratches down one cheek.

She stretched up to lay her hand against his face, just below the small abrasions. "She got you."

Hugh stilled, his eyes so blue they defied description. "Um, actually the rosebush did. But I'll live."

Though no five-o'clock shadow was visible on his face, the skin under her fingers was just rough enough to hint at the beginnings of stubble. Without thinking, she moved her thumb, tracing it lightly over his jaw.

"Joss."

She wasn't sure what he'd intended her name to be. A warning, a plea, a reminder? She had clear memories of his sighing her name, of his calling it out as he moved inside her.

There was a small moan, and she realized it had been hers. Then Hugh leaned in, his lips covering hers, and the next sound she made was absorbed by their kiss.

10

KISSING HUGH only seemed to get better—and that was saying something. He sucked at her lower lip, traced the curves of her lips with his tongue, exploring at a leisurely, sensual pace. When he finally entered her mouth, brushing his tongue against hers, moving in a slow, deliberate rhythm, Joss was damp with need. She tunneled her hands through his hair, wanting to be closer, wishing their bodies were fused together as intimately as their lips.

Bracing his weight with his arms alongside her on the couch, he lowered himself next to her. Hot shivers of pleasure traveled round-trip up and down her body, making regularly scheduled stops at her breasts and thighs. To make more room for him and to keep her ankle out of the way, she turned sideways, facing him, losing herself in the endless kiss.

Pharmacists should market Hugh. One touch of his lips, and a girl felt no pain at all—only a pulsing desire that was as enjoyable as it was insistent.

She murmured in wordless encouragement when he pulled her waist closer to his. Despite their fervent kisses, she noticed he was trying to be gentle with her body, but when she nipped at his lower lip, he ground against her and tightened his hold, momentarily forgetting to be tender. His tongue thrust against hers, and she thought she'd be happy to go on kissing him forever. But the phone rang before she had a chance to test that theory.

Her groan was considerably more annoyed than aroused; kissing Hugh wasn't a spectacular idea, but she'd been managing to ignore that issue until the phone dragged her out of the moment and into reality. "Bob."

Hugh sat back, his frown comical. "It would really help me here if you didn't say another guy's name."

She shook her head as she reached for the cordless. "If the call is for Bob, I'm throwing in the towel and getting a new number…. Hello?"

"Jocelyn. This is your mother."

Granted, they didn't speak on the phone often, but Joss still thought it was funny—or possibly sad— that Vivian felt she had to specify who she was. "Hi, Mom. What can I do for you?"

Thankfully, Hugh had stood and walked toward the kitchen. Coherent speech was a lot easier with his body in the other room.

"Actually," Vivian said, "I was calling to make sure you're doing everything possible for yourself. I ran into Stanley Patone and he happened to mention you haven't even called him since our brunch!"

Joss ground her teeth. No doubt he'd "happened to mention" this after one of Vivian's lengthy interrogations. "I plan to meet with him, Mom, but things have been crazy. My job situation's changed a little, and—"

"Don't tell me you're working for another felon."

Panic tinged Vivian's voice. "I don't know how I'd be able to face anyone at the club."

"No, nothing like that. The company went through a merger. Everyone from Visions is with Kimmerman and Kimmerman—"

"And I'm only just hearing about this *now?* Jocelyn, why didn't you call me? How would it have looked if I'd heard about this from someone else, when my own daughter works there?"

"I'm sorry, Mom. I've been…" Her gaze strayed to Hugh, who had opened a cabinet in the kitchen. "Preoccupied."

When he noticed her attention, he mouthed, "Glasses?"

"Cabinet to the left of the sink," she said softly.

"I beg your pardon?"

"Not you, Mom. I have a friend over."

"I thought your house wasn't ready for entertaining yet."

"It wasn't a scheduled visit. He drove me home because I had an accident earlier today. Nothing serious," she hastened to add, lest her mother think accident meant something in the motor-vehicle milieu. "I just sprained my ankle playing tennis."

Her mother clucked her tongue. "And after all that money we put into tennis lessons."

Joss really should've asked for a stronger pain prescription. "Mom, I have to go. But I promise, I will set up an appointment this week to see…" She cast another glance in Hugh's direction, not wanting to discuss Patone, since they were both vying for the man's business.

"You sound awfully flighty tonight," Vivian observed. "I hope whoever this 'friend' is, he isn't a

distraction. You have to stay focused to succeed, Jocelyn. If you can't rely on yourself, you—"

"Can't rely on anyone. I know. I'll talk to you later,
Mom." As Joss was disconnecting, the doorbell rang,
and Hugh disappeared into the foyer. Whatever else
could be said about Vivian—*oh, don't even get me
started*—she was still often right. Joss was definitely
"distracted."

Joss had told herself not half an hour ago that
Hugh wasn't the right person to trust with her heart,
if such a person even existed, yet she'd let herself get
so lost in his deep blue eyes and fantastic lips that if
her mother hadn't called Joss would even now be
looking for a sexual position that didn't cause her
ankle additional discomfort.

She and Hugh were not good for each other...wit-
ness today's rivalry and tonight's unsettling mixed
emotions. She'd worked hard all her life, but not even
her customary one hundred and ten percent was
helping her keep her hands off of him. In fact, when
she thought about exactly where she'd wanted to put
her hands—and where she'd wanted him to put
his—her face flamed. Now what?

Hide under the couch? No, not enough room.

Feign painkiller-induced sleep? No, she was far
too tense to fake a state of relaxed unconsciousness
with her heart racing this hard.

Answer all of his comments with "que, señor?"
and pretend not to speak English? No, this wasn't a
badly written sitcom.

That only left facing the truth, and she didn't
know which would be worse—being the one to say
that it had been a mistake, or hearing it from Hugh.

He walked back into the room, bringing with him the mouthwatering aroma of spicy tomato sauce and freshly baked dough. And the temptation to start making more mistakes. He set the cardboard box on the kitchen table, then came toward her.

He stopped a few feet away and slid his hands in the pockets of his shorts. "Joss—"

"There are clean plates in the dishwasher."

"What?"

"And you already poured yourself a drink, right? 'Cause there are sodas in the refrigerator."

"Joss, I don't want anything to drink. I want—"

"There's just no good way to end that sentence," she said softly. "Except possibly 'the Cowboys to get to the Super Bowl this year.' But even then, I'd probably be offended that you're thinking about football right now."

"Trust me, I'm not."

Trust him? Easier said than done.

"I've missed you," he told her.

A warm flutter of pleasure beat in her chest, but she did her best to ignore it. Maybe he'd just missed the physical relationship they'd shared. You'd have to be dead not to miss that.

"We work together," she reminded him.

"That didn't stop us before."

As arguments went, it wasn't his most convincing. "Yes, and didn't that turn out swimmingly?"

"It could have," he protested. "If you'd just—"

She narrowed her eyes.

He wisely dropped the issue, choosing instead to find plates and pull out a couple slices of hot pizza for the two of them. He ate his so quickly that he probably burned his mouth too badly to kiss anyone in the near future. The thought was selfishly comforting.

Once he'd finished, he returned his dishes to the kitchen, then hovered in the hallway. "I guess I should go?"

As opposed to stay and have delicious sex? "You really should. I'd see you out, but…"

"You need to stay off that ankle."

True. But what she'd really been thinking was that her knees might still be too weak from his kisses for her to stand.

"THERE ARE MORE embarrassing things," Emily comforted Joss from the armchair she was perched in. "After all, *he* kissed *you*. And you were caught up in that whole former lover chemistry. Plus, you were under pharmaceutical influence! It's not like you impulsively asked him out only to learn he was happily committed to his 'life partner'…. I am never inviting another man to dinner again."

Joss sipped the soda Emily had poured for her, carefully not smiling at her friend's expense.

Emily had come over to help out that morning, as soon as she'd learned of Joss's injured ankle. Once she'd arrived, Em shared the story of what had happened yesterday when she'd decided to be proactive with the research librarian and ask a man out for the first time. First and, apparently, last.

"At least when I had crappy judgment about men before," Emily grumbled, "they were straight men."

"There's still my semineighbor, Paul," Joss said encouragingly. "I saw him again Friday when he was out jogging. He's very sweet and definitely single. I managed to work you into conversation, and he reacted like an interested, straight guy."

"You swear he's cute?"

"As a button."

"Is the comparison to a clothing fastener really supposed to motivate me to shave my legs for the guy?"

Joss laughed. "He's good-looking, I promise."

Of course, he was no Hugh... *Not this again.* Hadn't she given her hormones a stern talking-to around midnight? And then again at about two in the morning when she'd been tossing and turning? And at a quarter after three?

She hadn't been able to sleep because of her throbbing...ankle.

Somebody should be having great sex, and if, for the moment, it wasn't going to be her, then it should definitely be Emily. "You know what I could do? Have a party!"

Emily looked at her blankly.

"I'll throw myself a housewarming." She wasn't sure if her reflexive horror at actually hosting guests in her unfinished home was the result of Vivian's comment the night before or simply her upbringing. The social events of her childhood had either involved fine china or meticulously planned "fun" themes for Joss's birthday parties, which had been attended mostly by the children of Important People. "I've sort of figured out Paul's jogging schedule, and I think I can work it out so I end up casually inviting him."

"You may be the first woman I've met who's stalking a guy she doesn't even want for herself," Emily teased.

"This isn't stalking, it's strategizing. I'll get a

few steaks for the grill, invite a couple of people from work…"

"You mean like that receptionist you've been trying to befriend?"

"No. I've…changed my mind about that." She would have said *given up* if it were in her vocabulary. "On Friday, I tried—"

The phone rang, and Joss tensed. It was likely that Hugh would want to check on her, wasn't it? See how her ankle was healing? Or maybe their interlude last night had stayed on his mind the way it had hers. She grabbed the cordless phone off of the end table. "Hello?"

"Yes, may I speak with Bob Becker please?" a woman asked.

Joss sighed. "Sorry, Bob's no longer at this number."

"Oh. I apologize for disturbing you."

"No problem." Joss disconnected, unable to deny the bolt of disappointment that had shot through her at the sound of a female voice. Not that she had the first clue what she would've said if it *had* been Hugh.

Em grinned. "How long do you think you're going to keep getting calls for that guy?"

"I have no idea." Joss was more concerned with how long she was going to be foolishly hung up on a completely different guy.

FINALLY. JOSS SAT BACK in her chair, calmly ecstatic that something had gone right this week…even if she'd had to wait until Thursday for that to happen. She'd spent Monday and Tuesday working from home, frustrated with her lack of mobility and the sense that she was avoiding Hugh, despite her very valid ankle excuse. Then yesterday, she'd been on-site with a difficult client who'd made her want to pull her hair out—wasn't there a way to keep customers away from the commercial shoots they were paying for? It hadn't helped that the director was a prima donna who'd muttered every few seconds "This is what I get for selling out," and threatened to walk off the set and go film the indie movie of his heart.

Yet, finally, this morning, seated in a small conference room decorated with bronzed hammers and saws mounted on the wall, things had taken a turn for the better. The way Stanley Patone beamed at her from across the polished oval table made it clear he was pleased, but even before studying his expression, she'd known she'd nailed her presentation, no hardware pun intended. As she'd been speaking, she'd experienced that euphoric almost out-of-body certainty that came from being so into what she was doing, so "on," that there was no room for extra thought or doubt.

It had been the same feeling she'd had while acing her SATs, when her subconscious had taken over for her, and she'd felt free to relax and watch herself sprint toward victory. The same feeling she'd had in high school when the first guy she'd ever noticed, and wanted to notice her, moved in to kiss her for the first time. Of course, when Hugh Brannon kissed her, it was a different sensation altogether. When his lips touched hers, her entire body sizzled and she—

Now is really not the time to think about that, Jocelyn.

Luckily, her hormones could reschedule. She knew this because, based on the last few days, she'd probably be thinking about Hugh again in an hour. If not sooner.

"That was wonderful," Stanley praised, mercifully interrupting her thoughts. "Some fresh, unique ideas without thumbing your nose at the tried and true. I'm ready to sign, just as long as Robert keeps my account in your hands."

Yes! It was the first new client she'd officially secured in her two weeks at Kimmerman, although she was making progress with several other companies. Call her instant-gratification girl, but she preferred victories over intangible "progress."

"I have a copy of the contracts in my briefcase for you to look over," Joss said, "but of course Mr. Kimmerman will want to finalize individual specifics. I look forward to our working together. You have a great product and service record, and I can't wait to let more of the public know about it."

He stood, wiping the traces of a jelly-filled doughnut from his fingers before shaking her hand. "Vivian was right to brag about you."

The comment caught her off guard and it took her a moment to produce a response. "Thanks."

Though she knew he'd meant well, Stanley's comment put a damper on her triumphant mood. Why was it that when she was *alone* with her mom, Joss could do no right, yet when Vivian spoke to others, all she did was play up her daughter's achievements? Was Vivian legitimately proud of Joss, or did having a successful daughter just make her look better as a mother?

"She'll be happy to know we're going with you," Stanley added.

Joss tilted her head. His tone made that sound like more than a casual remark, and she thought about her mother's uncharacteristic phone call over the weekend. "Do you and my mother talk often?"

He sighed. "Not nearly as often as I'd like."

Oh, the poor man. He had a crush on Vivian.

When she'd been younger, Joss hadn't paid much attention to her mom's lack of dates. Viv had such a powerful personality that it had really been enough for two parents. But as Joss had started to become interested in boys herself, finally noticing how absent her mother's love life was, she'd suspected Vivian was simply too busy with her own ambitions to make time for romance.

Or was it just that no man existed who lived up to Viv's demands? Joss knew from personal experience how exhausting it was to try. Amiable Stanley Patone, with his jelly-smudged fingers and beginnings of a comb over, just didn't seem her mother's type.

An unpleasant thought occurred to her—Stanley wasn't signing with Joss as an excuse to talk to or please Vivian, was he? *She'll be happy to know…* Nah, that was ridiculous. He was a businessman, and Joss had done a hell of a job. She'd given the presentation her all. Of course, this was the same "all" that had been resulting in recent trips to the emergency room and not one, but two, ill-advised instances of kissing Hugh Brannon.

But that had all been before today and the remembered feeling of what it was like to succeed, to not need anyone else. It might be true that everyone makes mistakes, but that didn't mean she had to *keep* making them.

"Excuse me?" Joss blinked, wondering if she'd misheard Kimmerman…*hoping* she'd misheard.

"You and Hugh should go together," her boss repeated, grinning at his own brilliance. "In fact, I had my secretary page him. He should be along any second."

That didn't give her much time to change Robert's mind. "But, sir, I—"

A knock at the door interrupted her, cutting off what would have been a very persuasive argument. Or at least very heartfelt groveling.

"Come in," the president called cheerfully.

Oh, sure. *He* could afford to be jovial. He wasn't the one being sent out of town with a colleague he'd been sucking face with a few days ago.

Hugh entered the office, drawing up short when he saw Joss. "Hey. I didn't realize you were in today. I thought you might still be…" *Hiding from me,* his laser-blue gaze said. "Recovering."

Why was her pulse pounding so hard? True, this was the first time she'd seen him since they'd made out on her couch last weekend, but that hardly had been the first time she'd made out with Hugh. Just last week, he'd kissed her in the parking lot of the hospital, and while she would have been lying if she'd said that had left her unaffected, it hadn't reduced her to feeling all trembly and uncertain inside every time she saw him afterward, either.

Maybe the difference was that after he'd kissed her at the hospital, they'd both acknowledged it was a mistake. When he'd kissed her Saturday, he'd seemed to think they—

"No." She shook her head. "Not at home today. I'm all better, feeling fine."

"As well she should be," Kimmerman interjected. "Joss here just signed Patone Power Tools."

Until Kimmerman said it out loud, she hadn't actually given any thought to the fact that she'd just officially won the client both she and Hugh had been courting. Odd, considering their competitive past.

"Congratulations," Hugh offered, but his expression was inscrutable.

Robert gestured for Hugh to have a seat. "There was never any question, of course, that Patone would become part of the Kimmerman family. Particularly with Stanley's relationship to Vivian McBride."

"What?" Joss hadn't actually meant to raise her voice loudly enough to be heard on the accounting side of the building. "I'm sorry. Just that…what relationship are you referring to, exactly?" *Oh, please, Lord, let it be that my mother is helping the man find a new house.*

Kimmerman leaned back in his leather chair, his eyebrows winging up in surprise. "They're a cute couple—unlikely but cute. I saw them having dinner at the club, and there was even that photo of them in the paper. At the opera fund-raiser, you know."

No. She hadn't.

Joss's eye twitched. She'd assumed Stanley's crush had been one-sided. How nice that her boss knew more about Joss's mother than Joss herself…and that Vivian had more of a social life than her daughter.

"And I'm hoping for similar success," Kimmerman said, "with Lynwood Fitness Equipment. Which is why I'm sending both of you to Houston."

"What?" Thank goodness the surprise had been Hugh's that time. She'd had her share for the morning.

"All the more to suck up to Lynwood," Kimmerman reasoned. "He's feeling slighted by the lack of attention his current agency gives him, so what better way to get him to consider us than to send not one but two of my best people to meet with his? I've got plenty of good execs, but you both have personal advantages for this particular courtship. Let's make a preliminary strike to get a feel for their needs. You two report back to me, and if we decide the expense of mock-ups is justified, I'll put everyone to work on campaign ideas, but the money in our spec budget doesn't grow on trees."

"When do we leave?" Judging from his even tone, Hugh had adjusted to the idea of this little trip better than she had.

"Next Tuesday," Kimmerman said. "You'll stay overnight and come back the following day."

Joss couldn't imagine in what parallel universe her going away with Hugh overnight was a good idea, but maybe Annette could arrange for them to stay on separate floors. All Joss had to do was hint at wanting a room close to Hugh's.

When their meeting with Kimmerman ended, Hugh held the door open for her, and she walked into the hall.

"You look like you're getting around pretty well." He ran his eyes over her in a completely nondiagnostic manner that left her with the same warm, pleasant, tingly light-headedness as a really good glass of wine. "Ankle healed, then?"

She nodded. "I'm not running any marathons, but I'll be fine. Thanks again for…your help the other night."

It had been nice of him to spend his afternoon stuck waiting in the E.R. with her. Now that she thought about it, both times they'd kissed had been after time spent at the hospital. She blamed the noxious pine-ammonia cleanser that permeated the place. Mind-altering fumes.

An awkward pause passed. Joss supposed she could always just walk away to end the moment, but that might not help, considering he was headed in the same direction.

He spoke first. "Congratulations again on signing Patone."

Was she imagining the wry accusation in his voice?

"I had no idea he was seeing my mother." She recalled Stanley's hangdog expression. "In fact, I'm not even sure that's true."

Hugh rolled his eyes. "Oh, come on. I saw them at that brunch, remember?"

Vivian had fawned over the power-tool mogul, true, but Joss's mother sucked up to anyone with money. It was not a reliable indicator of romantic interest. Although, looking back, Joss's mother really had put the "Viv" in *vivacious* that day. She'd spun amusing anecdote after anecdote, and had touched Stanley's arm or hand frequently. Joss had assumed the extra friendliness was an effort to secure business for her daughter—after all, Viv's philosophy had always been that she wasn't successful as a mother if Joss wasn't succeeding. But even if there had been a budding romance, Stanley's wistful expression earlier made her think it was over already.

Either way, she was good enough to have landed the account without outside help, Joss assured herself.

"See what it's like now?" Hugh asked.

She blinked, having no idea what he was talking about.

"The way people look at you when you luck into something, because of personal circumstances?"

"I didn't 'luck into' anything!" After all the hours she'd put into devising the perfect presentation for this morning, how dare he—

"Relax, I know you didn't." He winked at her. "*That* was my point. I won't deny that I've had some good luck—"

"But you've worked hard, too," she admitted sheepishly.

With a mock-solemn expression, he folded his hands together and bowed slightly. "You have learned well, grasshopper."

Her cheeks heated. "I'm sorry if I've implied you didn't deserve your success." It was just that she'd been taught if she worked hard enough for things, she would achieve them, only to discover life was not quite as advertised. Watching Hugh, who so often seemed to achieve more than she ever did with paradoxically less effort...

Suddenly, he reached forward and ran the pad of his thumb over her lower lip. She almost jumped at the unexpected contact. "You were frowning."

"Small wonder." Her smile was self-deprecating. "I *hate* being wrong." But maybe she had been wrong about Hugh in the past.

What about the future? Could they reach enough of an understanding that she could one day lean on him without first spraining a body part?

11

"I FEEL LIKE AN IDIOT," Emily complained under her breath, just loudly enough for Joss to hear her above the noise of ice being pulverized. With the blender running, there was no danger of one of the other three guests unintentionally eavesdropping. "Do they know they're here as camouflage to try to help me get a date?"

Joss glanced over to where Nick, Cherie and Lydia sat, chatting in her living room. Joss had just finished making the first round of Lusting After Your Former Lover Sucks Margaritas—the secret was in the sweet 'n sour. Emily was helping prepare a second batch of guacamole. The first on-line recipe Joss had tried had been an insult to avocados everywhere, and she'd been scandalized by her friend's suggestion that they could use a prepackaged mix. The unwitting guest of honor had yet to arrive.

"They are not camouflage," Joss insisted. "They're my friends. And so are you. I adore you and want to see you with a nice guy."

Someone around her was going to find a perfect relationship. Nick and Lydia were cute together, but he seemed too intent on impressing her by mentioning he'd caught "the game" on television last night—

though Joss doubted he even knew which sports were in season right now—and offering to fire up the grill for the ladies. Then there was the question of her mother and whatever was or wasn't going on between her and Stanley. Joss had almost picked up the phone to call Vivian and ask, but if her mom wanted her to know, Joss's number wasn't hard to find. All of Bob's friends stumbled across it easily enough.

When the doorbell rang, Joss turned with the expectant air of the village matchmaker. Glancing back in her friend's direction, she almost suggested Emily run to the powder room to freshen up her lipstick and straighten her curly ponytail.

Dear God. *I'm channeling my mother.*

Shuddering, Joss scooted away from her friend without comment and opened the front door. "Hi! Glad you could—"

Hugh raised his dark eyebrows. "I wasn't expecting you to be quite so happy to see me, but the enthusiasm's appreciated."

"What are you—"

"Found your sunglasses in the back seat of my car, and I thought you might need them back." He held them out to her. "Maybe they fell out of your purse."

From the back of the house, Cherie laughed loudly in appreciation at something either Emily or Lydia had just said. Hugh glanced from the cars in the driveway back to Joss, craning his neck in an attempt to see past her and looking entirely too interested in being invited to stay. She wasn't sure her libido was up for the unanticipated challenge of resisting him today, but succumbing to temptation mere days before their business trip had all the brilliance of telling a cute guy you'd just met that you were desperate for a commitment and wanted lots and lots of kids.

"Do you have people over?" Hugh asked.

"Yeah, a few girlfriends." Which was not a lie. "We're sorta having a chick get-together." Also not a lie, courtesy of the all-important *sorta.*

"Hey, Joss." Nick padded into the foyer behind her. "You wouldn't happen to have any more charcoal would you? Oh, Hugh. Didn't know you'd be here. Can I grab you a beer?"

Hugh's eyebrows zoomed up, and he spared a reproachful glance at Joss before looking over her shoulder to answer Nick. "A beer sounds good."

He wasn't really going to just invite himself in, was he?

When he sidestepped her and did exactly that, she followed, trying to figure out a way to throw him out on his fine butt without making herself look bad to the other guests. Why had he driven out to her house on a Saturday evening to return sunglasses? She had trouble believing the man didn't have dozens of potential plans for the night, and he was going to see her Monday, for crying out loud. Was he really that concerned about her having an optical emergency over the weekend?

Her party crasher stopped suddenly on the edge of the living room, and, unprepared for the halt, Joss smacked right into him. The red rayon shirt he wore was thin, and she could feel the solid heat of his muscles against her body.

He turned. "Throwing a little work get-together?"

Was she losing her mind, or did he seem a little

forlorn at being left out? Then again, it wasn't sur-
prising that he'd want to be in on any fun. "No, it's
not like that."

"Oh. My mistake, then. Guess I jumped to a wacky
conclusion based on our receptionist being here and
one of the staffers from the creative team lighting the
grill. And the redhead, what's her name again?"

"Cherie." Joss sighed. "She worked with me and
Nick at Visions, and I invited the two of them over.
Nick just happened to bring Lydia along." When the
doorbell pealed, she added, "Go get your beer. I have
to answer that."

Paul stood on her front porch, smiling and holding a clear plastic tray from the grocery store, the
kind that came with precut raw veggies and a tub of
dip. "Hi. Thanks again for inviting me."

"What are neighbors for?" She opened the door
wider, ushering him inside. "I'm just glad you could
make it."

He paused, a frown clouding his face. "I don't
normally do this, but something unexpected came up
today…. Is it all right that I brought someone with
me? You said it was an informal party, so I didn't
think one extra person—"

"It's fine." If the man had brought a date, they'd
hear her exasperated scream in Oklahoma. "The
more, the merrier."

Paul relaxed, running a hand through his sandy-
colored hair. "Great. My brother just unexpectedly
came into town this morning, and I didn't want to
cancel, but—"

"Brother?" As in there were now an even number
of men and women? Social serendipity. Except that

one of the men was *not* staying. She hoped. "No, I'm glad you brought him...um, where exactly is he?"

"Oh, Matt had an important business call just as we were leaving. He'll be along in a few minutes."

She took the veggie tray and ushered him toward the kitchen. Nick and Lydia were seated at the table, Em was pouring frozen cocktails into the margarita glasses she'd bought Joss for her birthday, and Hugh was leaning negligently against her counter with an air of casual familiarity that made Joss tingle. Cherie appeared to be in the rest room, where she'd probably retreated to primp once she'd taken a look at Hugh.

"Everyone, this is Paul Winchell, one of my new neighbors."

Joss experienced a twinge of satisfaction at Hugh's understated glare. Did he think the other man was potential competition? For a juvenile millisecond, she was tempted to cling to Paul's arm and perpetuate that myth.

But that would hardly further the Paul and Emily romance, and after repeated meetings with the man, Joss really did believe the two of them were perfect for each other. So she made the introductions.

"Hi." Emily smiled shyly.

"Nice to meet you." Paul smiled shyly.

Well, that was certainly a match made in...some place where people didn't say much. The good news was, Paul wasn't arrogantly speaking over top of Em the way Simon often had, as if she didn't have an opinion worth hearing. Maybe the silence between the two of them was of the instant connection they-heard-the-theme-to-*A-Summer-Place*-in-their-heads variety.

Joss picked up the plastic container in which she'd

been marinating steaks on the counter. "I'm just gonna slip outside and put these on the grill."

With any luck, Cherie would engage Hugh in conversation, and Nick and Lydia would continue to be engrossed in each other. That would leave Paul and Emily a chance to get to know one another. Joss opened the sliding-glass door and stepped out on the deck, but hadn't even had a chance to close it when she heard footsteps behind her. Turning around was unnecessary. The way her body softened and her breath escaped in an involuntary sigh told her perfectly well whose pheromones she'd sensed.

"What are you really doing here?" she asked as Hugh followed her outside.

"Thought maybe I could help with the cooking?"

"I meant at my house," she clarified, even though he'd known that.

He came to stand so close behind her that for a second she thought he was going to put his arms around her waist. "I had your sunglasses, remember?"

She shot him a pointed glance over her shoulder.

"Would it be better if I said you had my heart?"

Startled, she dropped her spatula. "Is that supposed to be funny?"

He rocked back on his heels. "Can I at least say you have my attention? My..." His eyes swept over the high-necked tank top she wore with relaxed-fit jeans. "Interest. I haven't able to stop thinking about our last kiss."

Her pulse pounded. "Try harder."

He set his beer bottle on the wooden railing, then raised his hand to her bare shoulder, his skin an icy contrast to hers because of the drink. It reminded her of the feel of cold ice cream against swollen, aching parts of her.

"Okay, you caught me," he said softly. "The sunglasses just presented an opportunity. I wanted to see if you were home tonight, wanted to see if *you* wanted to see me."

"Definitely." In all his naked glory—the sooner, the better. She cleared her throat. "I mean, it's good that you're here. Now there's an even number of men and women, which is always best, and if you stay after everyone else leaves..."

"Yes?"

Unaccountably nervous, she babbled, "Well, we never did discuss our strategy for the Lynwood meeting, and—"

"You want to talk about work." His hand fell away from her. "That figures."

His flat, critical tone hurt more than she would have expected, and she was grateful when the sliding-glass door made a scraping sound as the wheels ran across the metal runners, heralding an interruption.

"Joss?" Emily's tone was understandably startled. The situation probably looked intimate to anyone who didn't know better, or had eyeballs.

Hugh stepped back. "I was just offering my help with the food."

"Mmm-hmm." Emily crossed her arms over her chest, her smile skeptical and her stance uncharacteristically defiant. She was shy, but she wasn't an idiot.

Joss stole a glance at Hugh, at his disappointed, faintly disdainful expression.

"I should be going," he told her.

"You don't have to." Ten minutes ago, she would've applauded the idea.

"I really do. It's been a long week, and Saturday's the perfect opportunity to kick back at home and *relax*." He lifted his bottle in mock salute. "Thanks for the drink, though."

He walked into the house, and they could hear the muffled sound of conversation as he exchanged goodbyes. Joss sagged against the deck railing, both relieved and disappointed that he was going.

"Wow," Emily said. "You two generated more heat than the grill. Are you getting back together?"

"No, but I thought…I don't know what I thought." And she was increasingly less certain what she wanted.

Life without Hugh was so much more clear-cut. Joss had dated, but she didn't have vast experience with love. She'd certainly never fallen as fast for another man as she had for Hugh. Their breakup had hurt, and she would just as soon not relive that pain. If she got close to him again, only to have things end badly, it would feel worse than before.

Joss tilted her head. "So, did you come out here just to rescue me?"

"Hmm? Oh, no…I sneaked out for a second to say that Paul's just as cute as promised. Nick was talking about music, and it turns out Paul and I have an almost identical CD collection."

Joss was glad they were hitting it off, but her response was interrupted by the sound of a revving motorcycle engine cutting noisily through the peaceful Saturday evening. As the rumble got closer, Joss realized the motorcycle was actually coming down her driveway. She and Emily exchanged puzzled glances.

They went inside, making it to the kitchen just in time to see Paul offer a beer to a burly giant of a man in jeans and a Harley-Davidson T-shirt with the sleeves cut off. He had an intricate barbed-wire tattoo encircling one bicep, with a single closed rose cutting through it in the direction of his elbow.

"Joss." Paul beamed at her. "This is my brother, Matt."

She glanced from sandy-haired, pleasant-faced Paul in his khakis to Matt. "Right. I noted the, um, family resemblance."

Both men chuckled—well, Paul chuckled. Matt threw back his head and laughed the way she imagined Vikings had when they'd finished pillaging a village. Although, now that she looked closer, the brawny man with the neatly trimmed beard had the same brown eyes as her yuppie neighbor.

"We're half brothers," Paul added. "I was sort of the runt among my dad's kids."

That explained the five- or six-inch height difference, which might also be due in part to the steel-toed boots Matt wore.

He held out a calloused hand for Joss to shake. "Thanks for letting me drop in unexpected. I'm not gonna cause a problem in your dinner plans, am I?"

The man looked as though he could barbecue an entire cow and call it a snack. "N-no. We've got plenty to go around."

Joss noticed that Lydia and Cherie were both slack-jawed at the sight of their new guest. Nick was assessing him as if wondering where Matt fell on

Lydia's "manly men" meter. And Emily was staring at the guy's arm.

Noticing, Matt flexed his bicep. "I do some lifting."

Emily frowned. "Actually, I was looking at the tattoo. That had to have hurt."

"I've always thought about getting a tattoo," Nick said to no one in particular.

"I never understood the whole idea of defacing your body as a fashion statement," Emily added absently. Then she jerked her head up, shooting Joss a vaguely panicked, tell-me-I-didn't-just-say-that-outloud look.

Paul's eyes widened, but Matt just grinned. "I see you're wearing earrings. Pierced?"

Emily was already too busy apologizing to answer his question. "I'm sorry. I shouldn't have blurted that."

Matt shook his head in objection to her protest. "Nothing wrong with a woman who speaks her mind."

Paul and Nick hastened to agree in the roomful of women, and Joss steered everyone toward the kitchen and the snacks set up there. Trying to adjust to the stream of small surprises this evening, Joss wondered if her friends had saved her a margarita.

This is definitely not your mother's dinner party.

ALL DURING THE FLIGHT to Houston with Hugh barely inches away from her, Joss had assured herself that if she could just focus on business, on impressing Lynwood's brand manager, Keith Carter, the day would be a piece of cake.

Imitation chocolate, spongy aftertaste, disgustingly low-cal cake.

Though the current meeting was technically going well for her employer, she felt like a useless observer. On the plane, she'd tried to set the tone for their new-and-improved businesslike relationship by asking Hugh about possible presentation ideas. He'd pointed out that today was about getting to know the client's wants and needs so that Kimmerman and Kimmerman could think about presentations *later*.

"You're trying too hard, J. As usual." Before she could retort, he'd flashed that killer smile of his. "And if they do want some presentation ideas, we'll wing it. I work great under pressure."

Of all the execs Kimmerman could have paired with Hugh Brannon, loose cannon of the ad world, why had he sent *her*? She enjoyed "winging it" almost as much as menstrual cramps. Wasn't there something to be said for a well-thought-out, professional approach?

Apparently not, she decided as she smiled along with what Hugh was saying, occasionally nodding for Carter's benefit. The first fifteen minutes of the meeting, though liberally peppered with alumni nostalgia she couldn't participate in, had been fine. But then, just as the small talk was giving way to the real business, Hugh had conversationally stumbled into one of his spur-of-the-moment ideas. Keith had shown interest, and, ever since, Joss had barely been able to get a word in edgewise.

She almost wished she saw Hugh the way he used to be—so competitive that he'd been concocting solo-pitch ideas during their flight and was deliberately one-upping her now. Instead, she knew he was merely caught up in the creative process, overwhelmed by that same I-know-I'm-onto-something euphoria she didn't seem to be experiencing enough lately.

Today, especially, she felt off her game. While it was annoying that Hugh had barely paused for her to interject her few comments, in all honesty none of her contributions had been especially brilliant. *I have to do better.*

After she'd chosen to work for two employers who had now gone the way of the dodo and the dinosaur, she really wanted to prove herself at Kimmerman. Regardless of Hugh's earlier criticism about trying too hard, she should have come up with some great in-flight ideas, not spent the time stealing glances at Hugh's profile and watching him make faces at the baby in the seat in front of them. Then maybe Joss would be the one dazzling the client right now instead of feeling superfluous and confused about when her life had started to unravel.

12

HUGH PULLED THE RENTAL CAR into the hotel driveway, trying to calculate what he'd need to do to
smooth things over with Joss, who had been fairly silent since they'd left the Lynwood office complex.
She'd been charming and gracious when talking to
Carter, and Hugh had barely realized anything was
wrong until he'd seen her wounded expression when
Keith paused to take a phone call. In retrospect, Hugh
saw just how enthusiastically the client had run with
his ideas. He suspected Joss was less than ecstatic,
but, ironically, Hugh would have been more low-key
if she hadn't been there. Something about her goaded
him—whether it was his slight irritation with how
adamant she'd been that they have a strictly business
relationship, or simply his subconsciously wanting to
show off for her.

As they walked inside, he asked, "So what are
your plans for dinner?" Since she'd been about as
talkative as one of the gold-potted trees that decorated the skylighted lobby, he reasoned a direct question was his best shot at conversation.

Her stride quickened. "I thought I'd get room
service."

"That would just cost twice as much as if you had

the same thing down in the hotel restaurant. Why not have dinner with me instead?" He didn't want their day together to end like this. Though they would be returning to Dallas successful, Joss looked like a fan whose favorite player had been traded to an out-of-state franchise.

"Hugh—"

"We could discuss Lynwood," he coaxed, trying not to think about the fact he was reduced to luring a beautiful woman to dinner with the promise of shoptalk.

Regarding him skeptically, she folded her arms over her chest.

"Look, Kimmerman wants to sign this client, and I thought you were the type who gave one hundred and ten percent to her job." He really should be experiencing just a twinge of guilt for the way he was shamelessly pushing her buttons, but getting her out of her hotel room and inducing her to have fun was for her own good. "It's been a long day, though, and I understand if you're too tired to consider strategy tonight."

"You're *really* thinking about strategy?"

"Absolutely." Witness the strategizing he'd put into the conversation thus far.

"All right." She consulted her slim gold wristwatch. "I'll meet you here in about twenty minutes. I need to change."

Admitting it was a step in the right direction.

Joss STEPPED OFF the elevator, smoothing her skirt, suddenly wishing she'd left her hair pulled back instead of brushing it loose the way Hugh liked it. How had she let herself get conned into this? Knowing he'd been manipulating her hadn't stopped her from saying yes, or from trying to look her best. At least she could tell her conscience that it was a business dinner.

Whether or not her conscience believed her was its problem.

Hugh was waiting just outside the hotel's boisterous bar and grill. At the other end of the lobby there was a quieter restaurant with an award-winning menu. She'd thought they could eat there and come up with a unified recommendation for Kimmerman in relative peace.

Her dinner companion had different ideas. "Come on. I grabbed us a table."

"But…" Music from the live piano player spilled out of the lounge. "Is that really the best place to talk?"

"Relax. You worry too much." He reached out and took her hand, presumably to lead her inside, but they both froze when his fingers connected with hers. The contact was a tease, a simple touch that only whetted a rebellious appetite. There were far more interesting places on her body than her palm that she wanted him to explore.

She pulled her hand away, following him inside so he had no further excuse to reach for her.

"Don't worry, I didn't seat us near the piano," he told her, gesturing toward a square table to the left of an empty stage. The blazer he'd worn today hung over one of the chairs. "See, I thought this through."

To what extent? she wondered. He was all blue-eyed innocence as he pulled her chair out for her, but why had he pressed her to spend the evening with him? He'd claimed work—while that would have been true once, his priorities seemed different now.

"Hugh." She met his eyes, but quickly looked away out of self-preservation. Those baby-blues weren't going to help her regain the focus that seemed to be slipping lately. "Is this a, um, date?"

"Would you like it to be?

Yes! *You don't get a vote,* she admonished her hormones. "I think it's best that we keep things on a professional level."

"Absolutely…. Something from the bar?"

She raised her eyebrows as he handed her the small laminated specialty menu for the bar's more potent alcoholic favorites.

"Relax. If I was trying to seduce you, plying you with alcohol isn't the approach I would take." His grin was wicked. "I'd—"

"I am not going to bed with you," she blurted, very afraid that if he shared his hypothetical seduction technique, they'd somehow end up with a live demo.

"Of course not." But his expression was so knowing, with a confidence that bordered on arrogance, that some of her irritation from that afternoon returned. Hugh was the type who gloated, even when he did it in a subtle, almost unconscious, manner, and it made failing around him even worse.

She ground her teeth as she thought about the meeting and some of the ideas she'd had since they'd left Carter's office. She could include them in her report to Kimmerman, which would be a second chance to succeed, but she wished she hadn't blown her chance to make an outstanding first impression on the client. Normally, she did a better job thinking fast on her Franco Sarto-clad feet.

"Joss? Everything okay?"

How should she answer? If she admitted her feelings about today, would he tell her she was just being uptight? She hated the sense that if she shared her emotions, she'd have to justify them, too. Hugh made her self-conscious in a way that no one but Vivian ever had, and, ironically, it was for two completely opposite reasons—not trying enough and trying too hard.

"Is this about this afternoon?" he asked.

He had to pick *now* to be insightful and attuned to her feelings? "I just wish I'd been—" less convincing in her role of window dressing? "—more involved."

Hugh flashed her an uncharacteristically sheepish smile. "I guess I monopolized the conversation a little."

The unexpected semiapology warmed her, and she grinned in return. "You passed monopoly and zoomed right on to little green houses and red plastic hotels."

He laughed. "It wasn't intentional."

"I know." But the accidental oversight was depressing. She didn't know which was worse, feeling invisible in front of the customer, when professional success was so important to her...or feeling invisible to Hugh.

Still, the fact that he'd not only acknowledged her feelings but refrained from trivializing them was enough to ease some of the tension she'd been carrying in her stiff shoulders. A perky waitress in a polo shirt came to take their drink orders and suggest the nightly specials. Then a busboy brought them glasses of water and some complimentary tortilla chips. Joss felt far more at ease than she had when she'd come down from her hotel room.

After their food had been served, the subject returned to work. At first, she thought he was going to object to her all-business demeanor, but she needed the safe topic. Besides, he had lured her on the pretext of discussing Lynwood, and after a few minutes, he seemed as engrossed in the conversation as she was. She found herself asking Hugh's opinion on everything from demographics to media venues. They were in the middle of discussing a particularly horrendous campaign being mishandled by one of Kimmerman's competitors when the shrill sound of microphone feedback rent the air.

"Sorry about that folks," a man said, making Joss aware for the first time that someone had taken the stage.

As the unidentified man in the green-checkered shirt made some sort of sound adjustments, Joss whispered to Hugh, "What's going on?"

He shrugged.

But her question was answered a second later when the man boomed in welcome, "As most of you know, on Tuesday nights we bring you the best karaoke in these parts. Y'all better come on up and practice, 'cause we're having our special annual karaoke-in-costume Halloween extravaganza this Sunday, with a thousand dollar grand prize and giveaways throughout the night."

His words were met with applause, the volume of which was startling. Joss glanced around at the packed room. She hadn't noticed how many people were arriving in the dining room. Truthfully, she hadn't noticed much besides her charming dinner companion.

A few moments later, a gangly man in a three-piece suit took the stage. He did irreparable damage to the song of some one-hit wonder band whose name Joss couldn't quite recall. The next act was a young woman who did an impressive job with a rock ballad. The volume level inside the lounge had definitely halted Joss's conversation with Hugh, who looked more interested in watching the succession of acts on the stage than returning to the subject of advertising.

She drew the line at a good-looking tone-deaf man who should have had the sense to pick something that stayed in a lower register than *Unchained Melody*. Wincing, Joss pushed her plate away. "Check, please."

Hugh glanced at her. "You don't want to stick around for the fun?"

The man onstage hit a note not meant for human ears, and she squirmed in her seat. The noise wasn't all that enjoyable, and she was half-embarrassed for the man. "Sorry, this isn't my idea of a good time. I can't believe none of his friends talked him out of this."

She could only assume that the booth of people whooping their encouragement and clapping were his "friends." Maybe they were all tone-deaf, too. Or maybe the man had lost a bet.

Hugh frowned. "You, on the other hand, would stop a friend?"

"I nee-eeed your love…"

She winced again. "With force, if necessary. I wouldn't let someone I cared about make a public fool of himself." Her mind vibrated with an electric twinge of déjà vu, but before she could place the familiarity, Hugh was speaking again.

"Maybe they 'let him' because he's having such a great time. Something, I might add, that would do you some good."

The criticism stung, but Joss told herself she didn't need Hugh's opinion of what would be good for her. Hadn't she'd come this far in her life without the benefit of his wise guidance? She had a good job—although it wasn't exactly the one she'd set out to have, and she was still uncomfortable with her new circumstances. She had a great house—or the skeleton of one, anyway, which she was doing her best to flesh into something sublime. But none of that stopped her from demanding, "Are you implying I don't know how to have fun?"

He merely lifted his eyebrows in a pointed silent answer.

"I was having a party at my house on Saturday," she reminded him, chagrined that she felt the need to defend herself.

"Yeah, but there was something suspicious about that party."

"Like the sinister way I was offering people dip?"

He almost smiled. "I have trouble believing you blew off a day you could have been working on campaigns, or that house…. Not without a reason."

"Just kicking back is a reason."

"For normal people, sure."

And she was, what—a three-armed mutant?

Okay, *technically*, the purpose of the get-together was to introduce Paul and Emily, but that didn't mean all her relaxation came with ulterior motives.

Besides, watching the two of them get to know each other had been fun. They'd partnered for a trivia game late in the evening and won, and Emily had called yesterday to say he'd asked her out. They were probably out to dinner right now, in which case, Joss hoped her friend's date was going better than this one. Not that this was a date.

She pulled out her wallet. "I'm beat. I'm going to head up to my room."

"Right." He sounded resigned, and faintly disappointed in her. "I'm sticking around for a bit. Who knows, maybe I'll even brave the stage. I might not be Grammy material, but so what? How many of us can really sing, anyway?"

It suddenly occurred to her that he had no idea *she* could—she didn't publicize the fact her mom had been so embarrassed by her daughter's voice that she'd shelled out money they could've spent elsewhere on lessons. *Oh, hell.* She'd just pinpointed the source of déjà vu she'd been feeling moments ago. Joss had felt mortified for the poor man on stage, but he'd been enjoying himself. The way Joss had once enjoyed herself—out loud and imperfectly. Were there any traces of that little girl left?

She had an impulsive yearning to find out. Plus, her taking the stage would definitely knock Hugh for a loop. Now *that* would be fun.

"You know what?" She smiled sweetly. "I think I will put my name down. My bed will still be there when I'm finished singing, right?"

His jaw dropped. "This is because I dared you, isn't it?"

"Please, I'm not so juvenile that I make decisions

based on dares. Well, unless they're double-dogs, of course."

"A given," he agreed with a shrug and a bemused expression.

They approached the bar, and the woman behind it told them that there would be at least fifteen minutes before Joss's turn.

"Enough time for you to change your mind," Hugh said. It was difficult to tell whether he was trying to give her a gentlemanly out, or if he was just taunting her, unconvinced that she'd actually stick around.

"You don't think I'll do it." She fisted her hands on her hips. "Care to bet on that?"

"Nice try, but the point is for you to do something for the sheer hell of it, not to *win*."

His words had an oddly deflating effect. It was a scary look at herself psychologically, but she'd already been anticipating officially beating him and claiming some prize for it. She played it off. "Fine, but then you'll never know what exotic ideas I had for our wager."

His eyes gleamed with passion, and his lips parted. Then he took a deep breath, and met her gaze straight on…seemingly recovered. *She* couldn't seem to get the man out of her constantly overheated system, but *he* blinked away desire just like that? Now that was discouraging.

"What are you going to sing?" Hugh wanted to know. "On a scale of one to national anthem, you should probably stick to something easy. Don't be a hero."

Ignoring his yet again unsolicited advice, Joss

turned to the woman behind the bar and asked for a copy of the available song index. Hugh dragged a bar stool closer and perched himself on it, glancing over Joss's shoulder. She closed her eyes for a second, breathing in his cologne and wishing he weren't as sexy as he was irksome.

"'Don't You Want Me'?" he asked.

Her eyes flew open. "What? No!"

He chuckled wickedly in her ear. "All right, don't get all worked up. It was just a suggestion. What about...'Lay Your Hands on Me'?"

She glanced down to the list, which did indeed feature the old Bon Jovi single. "How about... 'Dream On'?"

Sliding his fingers beneath her loose hair and rubbing the base of her neck, he murmured, "'You Were Always on My Mind.'"

Mind? Must be nice to have one that functioned. Hers had gone walkabout the second he'd touched her. In a self-protective effort to shore up her defenses, she reminded herself that she certainly hadn't been on his mind today in Keith's office, when Hugh had acted as if she had all the relevance of an ornament.

"'Who's Sorry Now'?" she quipped.

The truth, though, was that whatever regret he might feel about their not being together, she mirrored it. Hugh wasn't a bad guy. He just got in a certain mode, one she knew pretty well, because she was constantly trying to find it herself. But even if he didn't bulldoze her deliberately, he drove her too crazy for them to reignite the flame between them.

He reached over her, letting his arm graze her

body as he idly turned the page. "Ah…here's a timeless classic. 'It Had To Be Hugh.'"

"'You.'" She sighed. "It's definitely *you*."

"Glad to see you stopped fighting your feelings and just admitted it, sweetheart."

She turned to glare into his impish blue eyes. "Are you quite finished?"

"I was hoping we were just getting started, but if you want to skip the song part and go up to bed—"

"Didn't I already make my opinion clear on that?" she interrupted.

"It's a woman's prerogative to change her mind."

Lord, she was tempted. The suggestive wordplay, the knowledge that at any time she could lean back the barest fraction of an inch and be pressed against a body that had brought hers to the height of passion countless times… She took a deep breath, trying to calm her racing heart.

Why did Hugh get to be so relaxed? Though she knew he was aroused, he seemed to be taking it in stride—a challenge to her inner competitor. Shouldn't he be flustered, too?

I can fix that.

"All right. I have my song," she said, returning the copy of the index to its rightful place.

"And?" Hugh prompted.

"Sorry, it's a surprise."

"After all my assistance, trying to help you pick something?"

"What can I say?" She smirked. "It's just more *fun* this way."

She shooed him back to their table, then promptly informed the woman at the bar of her selection. Afterward, Joss rejoined Hugh, but by the time her name was called out, she was second-guessing her bold impulse. She stood on wobbly legs.

This had seemed like a great idea when Hugh was goading her earlier. Now that she'd been sitting for a few minutes, cringing at someone else's performance…well, she wasn't in a vast hurry to be in the spotlight. She hadn't sung in front of anyone in years.

It'll be like falling off a bike, she tried to reassure herself. Or, wait. Maybe that should be like *riding* a bike. The latter might be less brutal and more encouraging, but, truthfully she was still expecting the former. Moving to a half-hearted smattering of applause, she walked up the side steps to the microphone.

"Let's give it up for Jocelyn," the evening's emcee invited.

His petition was met with a few more claps and a shrill whistle that Joss knew came from Hugh, though she couldn't see him clearly. She blinked against the bright stage lights, unable to make out anything more than a sea of dark blurs who were waiting. Waiting to judge her.

No, that wasn't right. She'd watched them cheer on other people who had absolutely no talent, just a desire to enjoy themselves. *Don't I have that desire, too?*

As the strong, bluesy opening piano chords to Norah Jones's "Turn Me On" played out over the speakers, Joss told herself there was at least one desire she had. It burned inside her every time her eyes met Hugh's, and she might as well make it work for her now.

She'd heard the expression "sing as if no one was listening." That was surprisingly easy to do since she couldn't see the people who were. Letting the steady beat ground her, she ignored the nervous breathlessness crowding her chest, urging her to rush and get this mad impulse over with. Instead, she took her time, swaying slightly—her body increasingly languid despite earlier tension—and followed the song's slow, sensual pacing.

While she couldn't see Hugh, she could feel him out there, watching her. She moved on stage as if he were the only man in the audience. By the time she'd started the second stanza, she'd given herself over to the plea of the song. Joss became each lyric, each simile, and she implored her absent lover to reappear and turn her on again. It was a relatively short song, and when she reached the end, holding the final sultry note, she was astonished to find herself finished. And trembling.

Thunderous applause erupted, making her aware of how much of herself she'd just revealed to a crowd of strangers. Her face flushed, Joss hurried off the stage. Maybe the majority of the packed house believed she'd just been performing a song, but she knew there was one person who knew it had all been Joss's naked desire for him, put to music and somebody else's eloquent words.

And when she reached the last step, that one person was waiting for her, passion burning in his bright blue eyes.

13

FOR A SECOND, JOSS THOUGHT Hugh might sweep her
into his arms, but then he shuffled back a few inches
to allow her room to clear the stage. She stepped forward, realizing they were in a shadowed corner.
Hardly alone, but everyone else's attention was on
the stage and on the new performers the emcee was
calling up, the evening's first duet.

She swallowed. "What did you think?" It wasn't
a cocky, guess-I-showed-you question, she simply
couldn't come up with anything else to say.

"What did I think?" He brushed her hair away
from her face, staring into her eyes. *Then* he swept her
into his arms.

His lips sought hers, and she kissed him back with
abandon, sliding her tongue against his. Thrusting,
retreating, exploring, savoring. Her ears rang, and
she couldn't think, could only cling and try to take
in enough of Hugh to ease her throbbing. But no half
measures were going to assuage her.

His hand dropped to the back of her skirt, cupping
her butt and squeezing appreciatively. She ground
her body against his, then broke their kiss long
enough to gasp, "My room."

He wrapped his fingers around hers, then tucked

her hand against him, guiding the two of them through the lively crowd. The lobby was bright and almost eerily still after the dimly lit energy of the lounge. Joss blinked away her momentary disorientation and quickened her pace. She wanted to get to her room. She wanted Hugh.

As they waited for the elevator, he avoided glancing in her direction, and she sensed from the tension in his body and the way his foot was tapping that he was too tightly wound for any extra visual stimulation. She understood completely. If *she* looked into his eyes right now, at his mouth… Her body ached in expectation.

Salvation came with a *ding* and slow-parting doors, and they hurried inside. When they were alone, safely away from any witnesses, Hugh used the hand he hadn't once let go of to spin her into his embrace. He dropped her fingers, shoving his hands into her hair. His kisses started at her mouth, but he gave that up in favor of nibbling her earlobe, then teasing the hollow of her throat.

They stopped on the seventh floor—a truly lucky number tonight, but not half as lucky as Joss was about to get. It took her two tries and several imaginative curses before she could get the key card to work, and then they were inside her room. She leaned against him, breathing in the scent that had driven her crazy whenever they'd been near each other during the past month. He lifted her straight up, and, despite the awkwardness of her skirt, she locked her legs around his waist as he walked them into the center of the room.

The mattress squeaked enthusiastically as they fell across the bed together, still kissing. Her earlier thought that she probably shouldn't reignite the flame between them mocked her. It had never gone out, and now it was a conflagration that seared away all her rational sensibilities. Rational was overrated. Her last boyfriend had been *rational*. Hugh was raw passion.

His fingers deftly worked the buttons of her blouse, and the silk fell away to the sides of her body. He turned his hand and brushed his knuckles over the lace of her bra.

"I've missed this body." He gazed down with rapt adoration. "I missed *you*."

She pulled him to her, and as they kissed he found the zipper on the skirt they'd crushed between them. He slid the material down until she could kick the garment free. He cupped her breasts, tweaking the nipples through the satin and lace, and the sensation shot straight to her womb. Her muscles clenched, and she felt wet and unbearably empty.

"I want you inside me," she murmured breathlessly, unzipping his pants.

He bit gently at the side of her neck. "Happy to oblige."

When he sat up to shuck his slacks, she helped him remove his shirt, as well. She sighed appreciatively at the sight he made—determined blue eyes, sexy half grin, tight abs and, straining against the cotton of his boxer-briefs, an erection that would inspire a girl to have sweet dreams for the rest of her life.

He lowered himself to the mattress with a tantalizing, predatory grin. Hurry, she wanted to say, but she was speechless with desire at the moment. Oh well, tugging at the waistband of his briefs should get the message across. His hands found her breasts again, and she arched into his palms, pointing her toes into the soft comforter.

"See how nice it feels to let yourself have some fun, J?" He sucked gently at her lower lip. "Should've listened to me a lot sooner."

His words were like ice cubes against her feverish skin—but not in the good way. Joss stiffened. "I'm sorry, did you just say 'I told you so'?"

"Um…" He did a one-armed push-up, levering himself above her. "No. Not exactly. Maybe a little."

Instead of stopping while he was ahead—or at least, not so far behind that they were in different time zones—he added, "You have to admit, I *was* right. You said we wouldn't end up in bed together. Rather vehemently in fact."

Sexy as he was, the man had never been able to resist gloating, and having her earlier words thrown back at her wasn't on her list of turn-ons. "You just don't change, Brannon."

"You liked me fine a minute ago." He sat up, his expression cocky. "Give me sixty seconds, and you'll like me again. We're great together. I can prove—"

"What? Prove me wrong, again? Prove that I'm too uptight?"

"You aren't exactly the picture of carefree joy, J."

Well, he'd killed that mood deader than dead— may it rest in peace.

She rolled to her side, gathering her shirt around her. "You should go."

"You're kidding me!" His incredulity was just so male. He honestly thought she was still going to have sex with him?

She took a deep breath, counted to ten and re-minded herself she did not want to strangle the man. Texas was a death-penalty state.

Even as he pulled his pants on, he tried to talk her out of her decision. "Joss, don't ruin both of our even-ings. You want this, too. What about earlier? The kissing? Onstage?"

With his shirt balled in her hands, she backed him toward the entrance of the suite. "I'm over that."

"Oh, come on. What about the song you chose? We both know—"

She opened the door. "Here's a song for your eve-ning—'All By Myself.'"

GROWING UP, Joss had been so apprehensive about screwing up that she'd obsessively tormented herself with all manner of unlikely karmic consequences. Yet, as bleak as some of her thoughts had been on the strained flight back to Dallas, she never could have predicted that after one little lustful lapse of judg-ment, she'd return home to standing water and cryp-tic phone messages.

Her answering machine informed her in its halt-ing, robotic voice that she had *four…new…messages:* looking for Bob, looking for Bob, Emily sounding anxious and looking for Bob. Joss picked up her phone and carried it downstairs, en route to the kitchen and the potential comfort food therein. Maybe she'd make mashed potatoes while she talked to Em—they were soothing.

Squish, squish. Uh-oh, that was new. She stopped in the hallway, glancing down, and her heart sank just as her footsteps had. When she flipped on the hallway light, she saw the puddle on her carpet and the water stains on the wall beneath the water-heater closet. Calling Emily suddenly took second place to tracking down a plumber.

Several hours later, her brand-new under-warranty water heater had been inspected by a plumber with official certification and semiofficial butt crack.

"I have good news," he cheerfully informed her.

"I could use some," Joss said from her seat at the kitchen table, where she was thinking there weren't enough potatoes in Idaho to salvage this evening.

He packed some tools into a blue box. "Your water heater is working fine."

"Uh-huh. Well, you're the one with the training in this area, but…"

"You had a cracked hose. And you'll probably wanna get new carpet. It'll be mildew central in no time."

Wonderful. One of the few places in the house where she *hadn't* planned to replace the flooring.

After the plumber left, Joss tried Emily again, but she got her friend's machine for the second time. She'd called while waiting for the plumber, but had been too disheartened to leave a message.

"I'm back in town," she said after the beep. "I'm also curious to know what 'Call me, Joss. And please don't be mad' means. Unless you sabotaged my water heater? Correction, water-heater hose. I hope everything's all right."

Joss had barely hit the end call button when the phone rang, causing her to jump. "Bob doesn't live here."

There was a pause so full of disapproval that the

person on the other end of the silence could only be Vivian. "What kind of salutation is that? Honestly, Jocelyn, I raised you with better manners."

Her mother. Naturally.

"I'm sorry, thought you were someone else. What can I do for you?"

"Well, next Sunday is the first weekend in November and therefore our scheduled brunch."

Why her mother was explaining this as if they hadn't been following the exact same pattern for years was a mystery, but then, so many things were these days. "Right."

"I thought perhaps you might be available this Sunday instead? Lacey wants to do a girls' weekend away for her fiftieth, and I won't be home until late afternoon or early evening."

"Oh." Her mother doing something as giddy as a "girls' weekend" was unimaginable. "This has nothing to do with a certain romance in your life?"

"Romance?" Vivian sounded even more appalled about that than she had about her daughter's phone etiquette. "What the devil are you talking about, Jocelyn?"

So…that would be a no, then.

"Never mind." Why was she relying on office rumors to keep up with her mother's life? *Because the two of you don't actually talk about your lives.* "Mom…"

What could she say after nearly three decades?

"Yes, Jocelyn?"

"Sunday will be fine."

"Lovely. Shall we meet at the Waif again? That was delightful."

Joss wouldn't have said delightful, exactly, but that Sunday brunch they'd shared with Hugh and Stanley Patone had been refreshing in one aspect—her clear sense of purpose. Win accounts for Wyatt, get house in tip-top shape, keep Hugh Brannon at cordial distance. Flash forward three weeks later: Wyatt was now in a different country; she'd just written a check for an obscene amount to cover faulty plumbing and she'd almost slept with Hugh last night. Not what one might call progress.

THERE WAS A KNOCK at the office door Thursday morning and Joss braced herself, just in case it was Hugh.

Although he hadn't seemed in a big hurry to see her again when they'd parted ways yesterday at the airport, she knew she would have meetings with him today. Everyone was getting together to discuss the mock-up campaign for Lynwood, and the creative team would probably be putting in overtime this weekend.

"Come in."

The door cracked open, and Emily peered inside. "Hey. I assigned my class a research day at the library, so thought I'd stop by for a few minutes. Sorry I didn't get a chance to call you back last night."

"I'm glad you're here." Joss shut the folder of Lynwood notes that lay open on her desk, giving Em her undivided attention. "I was worried. You left sort of a strange message."

"Yours wasn't of the norm, either. Sabotaged water heater?"

"Let's just say I'm considering the tranquil benefits of a kui pond…in my hallway. Less said about it, the better. Have a seat."

Emily complied, fidgeting with her hands and

staring all around the office, which she'd never actually been inside. Taking a good look at her friend, Joss realized that Emily's appearance was off, in small, subtle ways. Her hair was tidy enough, but she was wearing no makeup and a rumpled skirt and blouse. Then again, she didn't need much in the way of cosmetics with the spark in her eyes and rosy flush in her cheeks.

"I like your new office," Em said. "I know you were happy at Visions, but this is a nice setup. Scary department receptionist, though."

"Yeah, well. You know how some people seem a lot less intimidating and grow on you the more you get to know them? Annette's not one of those people."

Emily laughed, but then her expression grew more somber. "I wanted to see you to tell you about the last couple of nights. They've, well, they've been amazing…and completely unexpected."

Kind of like the night Joss could have had with Hugh if he'd known when not to talk? She squelched the unproductive thought. This conversation was about Em. "Sounds promising so far."

When her friend didn't volunteer any more information, Joss prompted, "So, Paul asked you out, and…?"

"He did." Emily sounded miserable about it. "We were going to meet at his house, since I had to run by and feed Dulcie for you, anyway. But when I got to his place he'd been held up at work, so Matt let me in."

"Matt?" The one who'd taken time out of his busy Hell's Angels schedule to drop by Joss's barbecue?

"Yeah, Paul's brother." Emily blushed.

Suddenly it became very clear to Joss where this was going. "Are you telling me you've spent the last two nights with Matt?"

Her friend nodded, but even with the visual confirmation, Joss couldn't believe it.

"*Matt?* Mr. barbed-wire biceps?"

"I know it sounds awful, and I certainly didn't mean to hit it off with Paul's brother. But sometimes chemistry just happens. You probably can't understand…"

Oh, I don't know about that. "I've been known to make the occasional gargantuan error when it comes to men, trust me. But you can fix it. You just—"

"It's not something I want to 'fix,'" Emily said with a gentle smile. "I'm crazy about him. I just feel bad for Paul, not that I'm breaking his heart or anything. Just that it may be a tad awkward at first, since he asked me out first, and now I'm dating Matt."

Dating? Joss had been out of town one night! She recalled all the times Emily stuck up for Simon simply because it was easier to be with the wrong guy than to be alone. "How well do you even know the guy?

"I admit, my feelings are a little sudden, but I know him better than you think." Em's tone was becoming defensive. "We stayed up and talked until four in the morning the other night, and almost as late last night. Sometimes the best things in life are the unplanned. Besides, I don't know Paul, either, and you wouldn't have minded my dating *him*."

"Yes, but…but…" The idea of Paul and Emily had just seemed so perfect, right down to the identical CD collection The idea of Matt and Em seemed surreal. "What does Matt listen to?"

"His favorite band is some group called the Parole

Violators. They're not as bad as you'd think, but it wouldn't matter much if they were. I'm not basing my future on the music he listens to in his car. Figuratively speaking. He doesn't have a car."

Basing my future. Bad sign. Whether Emily wanted to spend time with Paul or Matt or someone completely different, Joss worried about her friend jumping into something so quickly that it would hurt her in the end. Joss couldn't tell another grown woman what to do, of course, but what sort of friend would she be if she didn't try to keep Em from making potentially painful mistakes?

"Emily, we should talk about this more, maybe this weekend?"

"Sure. I'd love to tell you all about him, but Saturday's out. I have some stuff to catch up on during the day, and we're going to a concert at the amphitheater that night."

Joss didn't even want to know who was performing. "Well, Sunday morning I have brunch with my mother—Halloween with Vivian, insert your own joke here. But we could get together in the afternoon." Even though it would mean postponing her redecorating…again.

This was *not* supposed to be her life. Lusting after a co-worker who'd already threatened her heart once, talking her sensible and shy college-professor friend out of a relationship with a biker she barely knew. All these years, Joss had bought into the image her mother had extolled, that if Joss just tried hard enough, she would have that nifty house in the 'burbs and that lucrative, yet emotionally fulfilling job. How had everything disintegrated from a brochure-perfect existence to an alternate reality where Joss responsibly replaced her faulty water heater, yet *still* came home to a hallway she could water-ski in?

"I did try," she muttered, shoving both hands through her hair.

Emily leaned forward, her tone concerned. "What was that?"

"I said, I did try. I've been trying to fix up that house, I've been trying to make smart decisions about Hugh." Although her current record on that front sucked. "And I tried to help you find a nice guy."

"One out of three is a start. I have found a nice guy, Joss, which is why I came here to talk to you."

Joss sighed, thinking of all the times she'd wanted better for her modest friend than Em seemed to want for herself. "Oh, Emily."

"You know, there are some best friends in the world who would sound *happy* for me right now, instead of condescending."

Joss's head jerked up. She rarely ever heard Emily sound mad—even her anger at Simon when he'd unceremoniously dumped her had been short-lived. "I'm not being condescending. I just worry about you."

"Because you think I can't make good choices all by myself?" Emily stood. "That's condescension."

"You *asked* for my help," Joss managed to get out in a puzzled tone. "You said you'd been wrong about men once too often and that maybe you should just let me pick your next boyfriend."

"Well, I revoke the offer. You know what Matt did on our first date? He stopped outside the restaurant to flip a penny into the fountain and make a wish. I'm happy, you should be happy for me. Or at least turn your energy toward that house of yours and figuring out what to do about Hugh."

"Hugh?" She didn't need any figuring on that front. They were going to close the Lynwood deal together and work together very professionally and platonically. "There's nothing between me and Hugh."

"The funny thing is, you actually believe that. *You're* the one who needs help."

14

VIVIAN ORDERED AN egg-white omelette, but then drew her menu closer to her body instead of handing it over to the waiter. "You're *sure* the orange juice was freshly squeezed?"

"Y-yes, ma'am." It was the second time the gangly young man had given that assurance, after patiently listening to Viv's lecture when she first placed the order.

"I only ask because freshly squeezed juice has a certain texture, and—"

"I'll have the spinach quiche," Joss interrupted. The poor guy already looked as if he'd been interrogated for too long under bright lights and was ready to confess to invented crimes. A few more minutes, he'd be saying Viv's juice was from concentrate and claiming he was behind the Lindbergh kidnapping.

He flashed Joss a wan, but grateful smile. "Spinach quiche, got it." He took her menu, then made a grab for Viv's and sprinted off as though a getaway car waited around the corner.

"Well." Her mother pursed her lips. "You certainly ordered a rich breakfast."

Didn't matter. With Joss's lack of appetite the last few days, she probably wouldn't eat it, anyway. Even if she did, the extra calories would balance out against the two pounds she'd lost. Atkins had nothing on the quick weight loss of your best friend not speaking to you.

Emily had finally stomped out of Joss's office the other morning when the conversation had grown irreparably tense. After giving them time to regroup, Joss had tried to call Em on Friday. She didn't know if Emily had been home and avoiding her, or out with Matt. Joss had been upset enough that she hadn't had the necessary spare emotional energy to worry when Kimmerman assigned her and Hugh to copresent the agency's ideas to Colin Lynwood when he arrived next Friday.

Joss tried to shrug away her gloom, or at least her mother's criticism. "Could be worse—I could've ordered the bacon quiche. Much richer."

"I beg your pardon?"

"It's a joke," Joss mumbled. "I mean, it was supposed to be. You don't have to worry about my eating habits, I have a pretty good relationship with the food pyramid."

Vivian's carefully shaped eyebrows lifted. "I should hope so. I raised you to take care of yourself."

Oh, that was true in so many ways. The problem was, Joss wasn't sure she'd ever be able to let anyone else take care of her. And after her altercation with Emily, Joss wondered how her own caring translated to others. She'd certainly jettisoned her share of boyfriends over the years.

But none of that seemed to be what Vivian worried about.

I raised you to have better phone manners. I raised you to eat right. I raised you to succeed.

"All the times you told me to do better, try harder, was that for me, or to show what a great mother you were?" Joss said the words softly, not wanting to attack, simply wanting an honest answer.

Her mother sucked in her breath at the unexpected question—and it couldn't have been expected, because they rarely got that personal with each other. "You have no idea how difficult it is to be a single mother. I did a pretty damn good job. Look at how your life turned out!"

Bad example, Viv. Joss had recently begun to question how her life was turning out. "Mom, are you happy?"

"What a ridiculous question."

Joss sighed. "Could you humor me and answer it, anyway? I mean, are you ever…lonely?"

"Certainly not. I belong to several clubs, and Lacey and I lunch every other week."

"What about men?"

"I don't think I care for the direction of this conversation. Didn't I raise you to understand a woman can stand on her own without a man?"

"No argument there. But romance can be…" She had a scorching memory of Hugh's lips moving across her skin Tuesday night. "You can't tell me there haven't been one or two gentlemen who've admired you over the years."

"I couldn't indulge in flings. I had you to think about," Vivian said primly.

The comment didn't sit well with Joss. She felt guilty for ruining her mother's hypothetical love life, and, contrastingly, angry about the guilt. Joss knew it couldn't be easy to date and raise a child, but there were women who successfully did both. Besides, she'd been out of the house for a decade, presumably out of the way.

"What about now?" she asked. "You could go out with someone…like Stanley Patone."

Vivian stiffened, toying uneasily with the strand of pearls she wore. "Why on earth do you bring him up?"

"Because I think he cares about you, Mom. And he's a nice man."

"I suppose he is. But really, Jocelyn, is that the kind of man you picture me with?"

Joss bristled at her mother's tone. Vivian sounded so haughty and…condescending? Em had made the same accusation about Joss a few days ago. Joss had always assumed the "like mother, like daughter" adage applied to *other* families. Was she really so much like Vivian? Suddenly it seemed more important than ever to find the warmth in her mom's life.

"Maybe Stanley's not as polished as you are, but—"

"If you must know, I agreed to see him on several social occasions. He was amiable at all of them, but hardly my type. So you see, I gave him a chance."

Her mom's imperious tone set Joss's teeth on edge, and, instead of making the judicious move and dropping the subject, she asked, "A real chance, or did you just nitpick him apart?"

Normally, Joss wouldn't dream of talking to her mother this way, but so many sources of frustration had piled up that she could no longer find the inner balance that helped her stay calm and censor herself. Though there was probably a better way to have this conversation, finally speaking her mind was liberating—so much so that she'd apparently liberated her mother right out of brunch.

Vivian pushed her chair back and stood suddenly. "I take time out of my schedule for these brunches because you are my daughter, and I want to see you. But I did not come here to be verbally assaulted by my ungrateful child. So, if you'll excuse me…"

In her regal huff toward the entrance, her mother almost knocked aside the waiter who was bringing their food to the table. He didn't seem sorry to see Vivian go. Unexpectedly, Joss was.

JOSS WAS SITTING at her desk Monday morning, listening to the patter of rain outside, when a jar of green olives came into her office. Well, more accurately, a male hand reached around the corner of her open door, holding a bow-topped jar.

"They're for you," Hugh said as he stepped inside.

She squinted at him, then at the pimento-stuffed olives. "So they're… I give up. Your way of saying working with me requires martinis?" Emily and Vivian would probably concur. Joss still couldn't believe she'd let a rare fight with her friend put her in such a bad mood she'd picked an even rarer fight with her mother.

"No, no martinis." He laughed. "I got these because I couldn't find an olive branch."

"Did you try eBay?"

His dimpled grin was all the petition for peace he'd ever need. "See, that's one of the many things I adore about you—your great ideas. Joss, I know we haven't been on the friendliest terms. Or, maybe the terms got a little too friendly. My point is, I screwed up in Houston. Could we just put that behind us? I want us to be able to work together and come up with a presentation that will dazzle Lynwood. You really *do* have great ideas, and I swear I wasn't trying to shut you out at the meeting with Keith."

Her heart melted at his grand apologetic gesture. The fact that he was showing such empathy toward her feelings was delightful, and bizarrely ironic, considering the way Joss had recently hurt the feelings of not one but two of the women in her life.

How is it that, between the two of us, Hugh is the sensitive one? It was a world gone mad.

"I know you weren't trying to," she assured him. "You were just in your element, caught up in doing what you do best."

"You aren't irritated anymore?"

She shook her head ruefully. "My friend Em recently made it clear to me that I'm not such a picnic myself. And like you, all I really want is to do a great job on this mock campaign."

His blue eyes met hers, and, for a moment, she admitted there *was* something else she wanted. But juggling personal and professional relationships hadn't seemed to work between her and Hugh, even before her recent nosedive in interpersonal skills. Besides, after all the work Kimmerman employees had poured into the mock-up designs over the weekend, she owed it to the company to focus on Friday's upcoming presentation.

Hugh cleared his throat. "I'll let you get back to work, then."

She nodded, but as he walked out of her office, she realized work hadn't been as fulfilling as she'd hoped it would be when she graduated college. For a long time now, it had seemed that something was missing. Joss craved that definitive feeling of success, but between Mitman's scandal and being shuttled from Wyatt's group to K and K... *You're just frustrated with the lack of control.*

Or frustrated with all the other areas of her life.

As the morning's pace grew increasingly frenetic, she became too busy to dwell on anything but doing her job. She was in the midst of trying to explain diplomatically for the third time to the owner of The Little Bakery that a billboard with a pregnant woman in a white apron, captioned Check Out the Buns in Our Oven, was not the best way to go, when Annette beeped her.

Joss gratefully made her excuses to the bakery proprietor, then hit the intercom button.

"Your voice mailbox is full," Annette said in a scornful tone that made Joss think the woman had really missed her calling as an airport ticketing agent for EWA. "Did you want to take this call, or shall I write down a message?"

Heaven forbid Joss impose on the woman to fulfill part of her job description. "No, I've got it. Thanks, Annette... Jocelyn McBride speaking."

"Jocelyn, hello. I'm so pleased to have reached you." There was considerable static, but she could make out a man's hearty voice and unmistakable Manhattan accent. "This is Marty Slossinger."

Her mouth went dry. Martin Slossinger was legendary. He worked for one of the big-ten agencies in New York and had accepted more than one Clio award. What were the odds he was calling her to help with some regional work or client overflow? The prospect was enough to have her salivating again.

"Mr. Slossinger, what an honor to speak to you. I'm a big fan."

He chuckled. "The feeling's mutual. I really felt you deserved the ADster last year. Some of the radio spots you've overseen are genius."

Wow. If she'd known that idly wishing for a little career validation would garner her praise from Marty Slossinger himself, she would've sat in her office feeling sorry for herself long before now. "What can I do for you?"

"Don't be silly, Ms. McBride...I'm calling to let you know what *I* can do for *you*. You've heard of me, so I assume you're familiar with my employers?"

The agency used in a quarter of all case studies in marketing classes? "It would be safe to make that assumption, yes."

"Well, we'd like to fly you to New York, meet with you. I know that this is a bit sudden, but we have an opening, and our workload doesn't allow for a lot of indecisive pussyfooting. Our partners are all very impressed with you. Your work ethic is legendary, and you've recently been highly recommended by Shane Neely, from Neely-Richards. I believe you had a meeting with them just a few weeks ago?"

That meeting seemed as if it had happened in a previous lifetime, but timing wasn't the only surreal issue here. "Your company wants to interview me?"

"That's right. If you're interested."

Of course she was! "I'm flattered. But you were right about this being sudden. I'm in the middle of putting together a big client presentation this week, but could I get your number, maybe call you back when I've had a chance to think about this?"

"I tell you what, take a week, then let me know." He chuckled again, as if he realized this was sheer formality on her part. After he'd given her his number, he added, "Just remember—as we in the ad business say, the offer's only available for a limited time."

WHEN SHE'D AWAKENED that morning, Joss wouldn't have predicted that the drizzly, depressing Monday would turn out so well...or that Emily would be coming up the stairs to see her when Joss walked down the office corridor at the end of the day. Both women stopped in their tracks.

"You almost missed me," Joss said, hoping her friend's presence was a good sign.

Emily glanced from Joss's umbrella to her laptop case. "You're leaving before six-thirty?"

"I'm taking a lot of work home tonight." And she'd felt guilty sitting in her Kimmerman office thinking about what it would be like to work in New York. "I would've left earlier, but I couldn't get off the phone. Now I'm glad."

"Me, too." Emily shoved her hands in the pockets of the long raincoat she was wearing.

Joss was bursting to tell Emily about the New York phone call, but there were more important things to take care of first. "Emily, I tried to call you, but saying this in person is actually better. I'm sorry for the way I behaved last week. I'm sorry I wasn't more supportive of your relationship with Matt. All I want is for you to be happy."

Emily nodded. "I know, that's why I came here today. Ironically enough, Matt helped me realize you were just worried about me. I know not all of my dating choices have been great ones, but he's a good guy. And he was right when he told me I'd feel better after I talked to you. Your comments last week upset me, but I hate fighting with you, Joss. Let's not ever argue again! My weekend was wall-to-wall nervous eating."

Joss laughed. "So *that's* where my appetite went off to. I've hardly been able to eat or sleep. You know you're like a sister to me, right?"

"Same here. You're like the sister I begged my parents to exchange one of my brothers for."

Within minutes, the two women were talking in tandem. Emily confessed that while she thought Matt was perfect for her, they did need to slow down a little and give their relationship a chance to grow without rushing each other. Joss explained all about the fight with Vivian.

She wanted to tell Emily about the job offer, or at least the possible interview, but not here, when someone from Kimmerman might overhear her. Ditto on mentioning Hugh and his olives, or how unexpectedly moved she'd been by his apology. That had been one of her biggest complaints about the man when they'd been dating. It wasn't that he'd occasionally annoyed her, but that he never seemed to acknowledge her *right* to be annoyed.

"Walk me to my car?" Joss asked. "Or maybe do you want to grab dinner?"

"I do, but I can't tonight. Matt's going back to Oklahoma tomorrow. He'd never actually intended to stay this long, but then we met. And he wanted to make sure Paul was okay with everything."

"Is he?"

"Yeah, he's been really sweet. You were right when you said he was a nice guy. I think he was confused at first, but it's not like he was ever broken-hearted. He just wasn't the one. Don't worry, I'm going to take my time deciding whether or not Matt is." Emily grinned. "But all signs are promising so far."

They settled on lunch later in the week, then parted, each headed for her own car. Joss realized as she unlocked her door that she'd never seen her friend this happy. It was definitely time to cross Em's love life off her list of things to try to perfect.

Now, if I could just figure out what to do about my own.

"IN SHORT," JOSS SAID, "we feel that with our media know-how and your user-friendly product, we can let the world know what they've been missing in Lynwood Fitness Equipment." Projected on the wall behind her was her and Hugh's last slide—an illustration depicting a portly, frustrated-looking man on a treadmill, with the words Feel Like You're Not Getting Anywhere? Then It's Time to Try the Lynwood Fitness Approach written above him.

With the slide show concluded, Joss nodded to her partner. Hugh hit the switch near the door of the conference room, bringing the lights back up.

There was an immediate whisper of sound as all heads swiveled toward Colin Lynwood to determine his satisfaction—or, *gulp*, lack thereof—with the afternoon's demonstration.

He nodded, too much of a businessman to appear

overly eager with several agencies competing for his account. But his smile was promising. "I must say, you people do know your stuff. Jocelyn, Hugh, fine presentation."

Hugh had joined her at the front of the room, and he returned Lynwood's nod. "Thank you, sir, but most of the credit goes to Joss. She's the brains of this operation, I'm just the beauty."

A ripple of laughter went across the table, and Joss grinned. Earlier, she'd played straight man, pointing out the relatively dry facts in the booklets she and Hugh had passed out, setting him up for enough jokes to keep the meeting entertaining and upbeat. Lynwood might be all business, but Joss and Hugh had wanted to add some oomph to their presentation, to go beyond the numbers and figures of media markets, Arbitron stats and cost analysis.

We're a hell of a team.

The sensation was a new one for her. She'd known they were strong individually, but this was the first time she'd ever felt they'd truly meshed, bringing out the best in each other professionally. It was a surprisingly euphoric feeling, a different high than she got when she accomplished a task by herself. It had taken the argument with her sole living relative and the period of tension with Emily to make Joss aware of how alone she sometimes felt, despite her family and colleagues.

Not many people got close to her, so this synergy today was a new, heady thing. She'd always thought Vivian's birthday gift of a Siamese cat was typical of her mom—little personal regard for Joss's traveling lifestyle, expensive pedigree. Now Joss wondered if

Viv might be a little lonely herself and trying, in her own way, to keep her daughter from suffering that.

Without quite intending to, she started to extend her fingers toward Hugh's, then stopped in the sudden realization that she'd actually been reaching for his hand. But she couldn't help wanting to touch him, wanting to feel a physical manifestation of the connection that had flowed between them all day like the electric current in her old kitchen wiring—strong enough to catch someone unawares and fling them to the front of the house.

She brought her binder to her chest, gripping it tightly in both hands to help her regain control. Luckily, Kimmerman had stepped into the conversation, and all eyes were on the two presidents as they discussed what their respective companies could do for the other. Probably no one had noticed the sudden tremble in her hands and blush of color in her cheeks.

Except Hugh. His gaze slid toward her every few seconds, and even after they'd taken their seats and rejoined the discussion, she could feel his eyes on her from time to time. The connection that had fueled their presentation made her hyperaware of him now...and of his attraction for her, simmering just below the surface.

The other day, he'd said they'd just forget what had happened in Houston, no doubt believing that would be Joss's wish, too. But she realized she didn't want to forget. She wanted to finish it.

When the meeting ended and Kimmerman invited Lynwood to his club for dinner to finish their discussions CEO to CEO, Hugh sidled up to her, obviously trying not to look cocky, even though they both knew they'd bagged this one.

"Would you think it premature if I invited you out for a celebratory dinner?" he asked her softly.

She stared into his blue eyes, lost, with no desire to be found. *Just do it,* a voice in her head urged her. At least this one didn't sound like her mother. The Nike people, maybe. Vivian, no.

"Actually…I was thinking more along the lines of celebratory sex."

15

As Hugh waited impatiently for Joss to unlock her door, he thought that maybe his brother Craig's complaints about him had been right all along. At the moment, not even *Hugh* could believe his own luck.

He'd wondered earlier this week if continued pursuit of Joss was wise. After all, he'd known that she wasn't entirely conducive to the stop-and-smell-the-roses kind of guy he wanted to be—if guys actually did lame-ass stuff like sniff roses. In fact, part of the reason he'd been so gung ho during that meeting with Keith Carter had been an attempt to play at Joss's level and gain her respect. So he'd backed off.

Yet, now, here she was, tugging him inside her foyer by his necktie. *Life is good.*

The entryway was as far as they made it. Hugh guided her back to the wall, leaning into her, their mouths almost frantic. It had been far too long since they'd made love. Her tongue tangled with his, and he rocked his body against hers.

"Hugh," she muttered. "Light switch…ow."

It took him a moment to realize the lights were going on and off. And why.

He took a step back. "Sorry."

Mostly, he was sorry that they'd stopped, but she

took him by the hand and led him up the stairs. They shed shoes and jackets as they went. Her bedroom beckoned from the landing like an oasis, and not the cartoon kind where Daffy Duck finds himself spitting sand. No, this—Joss—was the real thing. He made a mental note not to talk this time and screw things up.

As soon as they made it to the bed, he began kissing her again, stopping only long enough to pull off her knit top before they hit the mattress. Her head fell back as he pressed his lips to the hollow of her throat, her silky blond hair spread across the pillow. Saying a quick thank-you to whomever had invented the front bra clasp, he easily flipped open the little piece of plastic and cupped the velvety mounds of her breasts. Her nipples were already rigid, seeking his attention. He laved first one, then the other, sucking hard on a peak, loving the way she clasped his head to her.

Her nails raked up and down his skin beneath the shirt she'd unbuttoned, and she writhed as he continued to kiss her breasts. "More. No more."

His laugh was hoarse and sounded suspiciously like a groan. "I don't think you can have it both ways, J."

"Don't do *that* anymore," she clarified breathlessly. A second later she added, "I don't want to come like this—still half-clothed and without you."

"Whatever the lady wants," he agreed quickly, removing the last of his clothes as she shimmied out of her own. He started to pitch his pants to the floor, but stopped to retrieve a condom.

Joss unrolled the latex over his almost painful erection. He felt himself jerk against her hand and he swallowed a moan. Eager to touch her, he rolled her over to her back, trailing his fingers across her belly, through the short soft nest of curls covering her. He parted the damp feminine furrows, and she sucked in her breath as he found her center, stroking his thumb over the swollen bud.

He braced himself above her and drove into her, pausing just long enough to savor the moment before moving inside her. She raised her hips to meet his, again and again, until he could feel a quaking start at the core of her, her muscles spasming in a tight inner rhythm that left her gasping his name.

Her own name was a soundless whisper on his lips as he climaxed in a mindless surge of pleasure.

He collapsed against her, loving the way her skin glistened with a fine sheen of perspiration. He doubted Joss let very many people see her sweaty. She wrapped her arms around him, not speaking but tightening her hold in a manner that made it clear she didn't want to let him go.

"Lynwood Fitness is a sham," she finally muttered against his chest.

He raised himself up on one elbow. "What?" Surely she wasn't going to talk business *now.* He needed to be with someone who knew how to relax and enjoy life—how to relax and enjoy him. Too often, he'd had reason to believe Joss wasn't that someone.

"We were supposed to make all those exercise options of theirs look like sublime physical activity," she continued, "but I'm sorry, *nothing* beats this."

"Oh." Relief rippled through him. "Well, I'm happy to burn your calories anytime, baby."

Her laugh gave him hope. She definitely sounded like a woman learning to let go.

"Speaking of calories…" He smiled down into her face, brushing strands of hair away from her cheek. "Got any butter pecan?"

JOSS LAY FLAT ON HER BACK, breathing hard and staring at the ceiling, wondering why she didn't feel exhausted. You'd think twenty-four hours of sex would wipe a girl out, but here she was, Saturday night, coasting on a swell of exhilaration. She supposed Hugh, sprawled beside her, would think it strange if she got up and went to finish painting her dining room right now. But she felt energized.

All right, so maybe the energy was mostly mental. There was a difference between *feeling* wide-awake and invigorated and actually being able to walk downstairs…or even as far as her nightstand. But her physical state of near boneless relaxation didn't stop her thoughts from flying around like glittery flakes in a shaken snow globe.

Unfortunately, some of those active thoughts were reminding her that she owed Marty Slossinger a phone call Monday morning, and her incredible weekend with Hugh wasn't making her decision any easier. Did she really want to move away from what she had here? If her answer was yes, could she find some sucker to buy the house-in-transition? On the other hand, what had she been working for all these years? Turning down some of the dates she wished she hadn't in school, to study and be valedictorian instead of salutatorian; working so hard to build her professional reputation…didn't it have to mean something, lead somewhere definitive?

Marty's firm was the best potential employer out

there right now. So, unless she wanted to go into business for herself, it seemed crazy not to seize this opportunity.

"You seem awfully serious," Hugh said without raising his head from the pillow.

"How can you tell? You didn't even look my way."

"You have very somber breathing. Is there something more I can do to help you relax?" he volunteered suggestively. "Once feeling returns to my body."

She grinned. "I'll see if I can come up with something we didn't already try today. But, to answer your implied question, I was just thinking about work."

With a groan, he threw his forearm over his eyes. "Why would you ruin a perfectly good weekend like that?"

"Would it make you feel better if I said I was also thinking about you?"

"Yes, but I want your thoughts of me to be the naked kind, not the three-piece suit. Unless, of course, you think of me in a three-piece suit and then imagine all the ways you could get me naked. That's acceptable."

She would have laughed if her spinning thoughts weren't starting to give her a headache. "Can you be serious for a second?"

"Can you not be?" He rolled away from her. "All *I* want to do is catch my breath and make love to you again, and you're over here...what? Worrying about The Little Bakery campaign? Lynwood?"

"No." Her future—where she was going and whether Hugh would be there. "Sometimes I consider what it would be like to start my own agency And I was thinking that you and I worked so well together on this last presentation…" The bond, not to mention the sex, had been amazing.

"Joss, you're not asking me to go into business with you, are you?" He propped himself up on one elbow to look at her, his expression giving new definition to appalled.

The Merriam-Webster's people are printing corrections even as we speak.

Did he have to look so horrified? She hadn't been asking him to co-sign a business loan right there, just musing aloud. "What bothers you the most?" she asked. "The responsibility of an agency, or working that closely with me?"

The man actually *shuddered*. "Hard to say which is worse."

He said the words casually, but that made the dull stab of pain in her chest even worse. "Well. Don't sugarcoat it on my account."

"Don't get me wrong, you know I'm nuts about you. But…I'd be lying if I said I didn't occasionally worry about us making each other nuts. Sometimes I think you're just too tense."

"Because I'm not lying there thinking about more sex, the way you were?" Despite her earlier serenity, she found she had more than enough tension in her body to stand up and start scouting for her clothes. "I was sharing random thoughts, but please, forget I mentioned it. I definitely don't want to go into business with you."

"You're taking my disinterest too personally. I wouldn't want to be in charge like that. I was a born salesman—"

"You're telling me."

"What I mean is, I'm already doing the part of the business I enjoy. I'm content. Why take on the extra stress of all the administrative responsibility when I'm having fun now?"

There it was again, *fun*. His new buzzword. She was glad the old rivalry between them didn't seem to be an issue, but what was with his recent life-should-be-a-party philosophy? If he didn't take anything seriously, where did that leave his feelings for her?

"Well, excuse me, Mr. Status Quo, for thinking you had the potential to do more," she muttered.

He stood, glowering. "This is exactly the kind of thing I was worried about."

Worried? Hugh? Since when?

"What do you mean?" she asked, finding it bizarre that she was having this conversation with a naked man holding a pillow in front of himself.

"You, looking for more, looking to *do* more. Outside of bed, I'm not sure I could keep you satisfied."

His sharp tone left her feeling defensive and more exposed than she'd felt when she was naked. "So I aspire to things. You think I should just settle?"

"I don't know what you should do." He sounded as if "seek professional therapy" topped his list of suggestions. "But I'd say your urge to perfect everything around you is a little manic. This house, for instance..."

"It's a long-term investment!" Besides, when she was finished with it, it would be far more homey than anything she and Vivian had ever shared. She wanted something that was tasteful but livable, nothing that was pristine to the point of sterility.

"And your friend?" Hugh challenged. "The quiet

one you were shoving Paul at the night I returned your sunglasses?"

She stiffened, her too-recent disagreement with Emily a fresh wound.

Hugh's shirt was on the other side of the room, and he hadn't located his underwear yet. But he yanked his pants up in one angry movement. It would have served him right to get something caught in the zipper.

"And what about Annette?" he pressed on. "If you were a little less 'helpful' with your suggestions about how she could rearrange files or set up her computer programs, she might like you more."

Joss could feel her face heating in embarrassment. Did everyone know Annette didn't like her? She'd honestly tried so hard.

Having crossed the room, he lifted his shirt off of her dresser. "I'm sorry. I'm listening to myself and part of me's thinking, Hugh, you're being an ass. I'm not trying to come down on you, J. It's just that I watched Craig do what you're doing—hell, it's what *I* used to do. Always looking forward, never 'settling,' as you put it. It almost killed him, and I'm not sticking around to watch the same thing happen to you. Or worse, to fall into it again myself. When I'm not careful, you have that effect on me, and I don't want to be in a relationship where I have to be careful all the time."

Joss was speechless. She'd had bad breakups before, but no guy had actually hinted she'd put him in an early grave.

He paused in her doorway, as if searching for the words that would smooth over what had just happened.

Yeah, good luck with that one, pal.

"I do care about you."

That was the most painful thing he'd said all evening. Hearing the man that she'd fallen in love with—twice!—voice his own lukewarm feelings in a faintly pitying tone… At least he'd made her decision about interviewing in New York a lot easier.

ON SUNDAY MORNING, Joss tackled renovations, determined to finish the dining-room walls, but by late afternoon, Hugh's accusatory words about having a "manic need to perfect" echoed in her head like a really sarcastic gunshot. Plus, her shoulders ached.

She went into the kitchen for a glass of ice water, and felt a surge of pride as she studied the new stove and beautifully papered walls. There was nothing *manic* about applying her own talents to make a nice home. Then again, if Hugh was really wrong about her, why had she recently had a similar fight with Emily, who was so nonconfrontational as to make pacifists look threatening? But the eerie resemblance between Joss's conversation with Hugh and her conversation with Em wasn't the real reason for the burning knot of stress in her abdomen.

No, what bothered her the most was that so much of what he'd said last night reminded Joss of her own words the last time she'd talked to Vivian. How could Joss condemn her mother for her attitude, then turn around and inflict the same treatment on others? *I'm not judgmental. I was only trying to help.*

The way Vivian had tried to help by paying for those tennis lessons and singing lessons, the way Vivian had stayed on her daughter's back about studying, until Joss graduated as valedictorian? Lately, Joss had been freaked out on more than one occasion by the thought of being like her mother. Maybe that wasn't as sinister a fate as she'd thought. Vivian wasn't an easy woman to be around, but perhaps her heart had been in the right place.

An hour later, in either a fit of insight or procrastination, Joss knocked on the door of her mom's condo, hoping Vivian had returned from her weekend with Lacey on schedule and hadn't yet gone out anywhere. Her car was in its allotted space, but that didn't necessarily mean she wasn't with acquaintances. There was a peephole in her mother's door, and Joss stood there awkwardly, wondering what the odds were that Viv would simply choose not to see her daughter.

It was only as Viv actually did open the door that Joss realized she had no idea what to say. *And this couldn't have occurred to you on the freeway somewhere?*

"Jocelyn! What are you doing here…and looking like that?" Vivian, of course, was dressed in wrinkle-free coordinating separates and sported full makeup. "Is everything all right?"

Joss ran a hand over the small paint smear at the top of her jeans. "Yeah. I just, um, came over on impulse." When was the last time she'd done that?

"Please, come in. I actually thought about you a lot today."

That was a surprise, and Joss couldn't begin to guess at her mother's thoughts. Had her mind turned in Joss's direction simply because today was their normal brunch, or had the thoughts been more of a must-call-my-lawyer-and-have-that-ungrateful-girl-written-out-of-my-will thing?

Joss walked in to her mother's Southwestern-themed living room. Sunset colors were in abundance—sand-and-mauve furniture with bright splashes of dark orange in the throw rug and vases. Some people's decorative knickknacks matched their personalities, but Viv's always matched her theme. Now, for instance, she had stunning photos of the desert hanging on the wall. A few years ago, the paintings had been abstracts that went with the previous sleek modern scheme.

There was only one personal picture—the two of them at Joss's college graduation. It hung in the hallway, a thematically neutral zone.

Vivian sat on the couch without offering Joss anything in the way of refreshments. She was either really pissed or nervous.

Joss took the chair next to the unused fireplace. "How was your weekend? Did you and Lacey have fun?"

"Mmm-hmm. We went to a spa, and it was nice, though I have no desire to be wrapped in seaweed again anytime soon. But surely you didn't drive all this way to ask how my facials went?"

The funny thing was, the distance between their homes wasn't really "all this way." Yet it had felt like it for years. "Mom, I'm sorry about the other day, our brunch. It's not an excuse, but I'd had a disagreement with a friend and I was in a horrible mood."

"Thank you." Her mother sighed. "I appreciate your coming over to tell me that Jocelyn, but...I think you meant the things that you said."

Joss bit her lip. "Maybe, but having been on the receiving end of pretty much the same comments this week, I realize there were better ways to state my opinions."

"Receiving end? Someone accused you of nitpicking them apart?"

"Actually, of taking my perfectionist tendencies to manic extremes," Joss said wryly, knowing she had a better chance of finding the Holy Grail than a speck of dust in Vivian's apartment.

Vivian laughed. An honest-to-God, no-holds-barred laugh. Joss couldn't imagine anything else shocking her more. "Perfectionist, huh? Can't imagine where you would have got that from. Oh, Jocelyn, I did my best, I swear. I wanted so much for you."

The affection in her mother's voice was unmistakable, if hesitant, and emotion swelled in Joss's chest. "I believe you. And…I'm grateful for everything you did, Mom." She grinned. "Why, just last week the singing lessons came in handy."

Her mother sighed again. "Maybe it was all too much, though. At that spa, I had way too much time to think about everything. What you said the other day, what your childhood was like. When I was younger, I wanted to be a good daughter. I know that by today's contemporary standards, that doesn't sound like much of an ambition, but my parents were so busy, so distant. I wanted to please them, get their attention and make them proud. When the wedding was humiliatingly canceled, I knew I'd never truly make them happy. I redirected my focus to being a good mother instead. But in the process I believe I've given you the impression that *you* don't truly make *me* happy."

Tears stung Joss's eyes. She blinked them back, refusing to let them fall, but they had already clogged her throat, making it nearly impossible for her to reply.

"I am proud of you, Joss," her mother said softly. "And I'd like it if you could stay for a while."

"I'd like that, too."

"Wonderful. Maybe we could even start seeing each other outside of the monthly brunch. I'm open to suggestions, especially ones that don't involve seaweed."

16

Joss was used to being able to pace while talking on the phone, but here at the office she was locked to her desk, so she settled for drumming her pen against her keyboard as she talked to Emily. She didn't feel guilty for spending the time on a personal call since it was only seven-thirty in the morning. Work didn't officially start for another hour, and most people hadn't even come in yet.

"Wow. I go to Oklahoma for a few days, and look what I miss," Emily said, her tone awestruck.

"I know. I can't believe that after all this time, Mom and I are *finally* getting along, just as I'm considering a move."

"Don't remind me. I don't know what I'm going to do without you."

"Hey, if you and Matt can make it work long-distance, you and I will have no problem. We'll just have very high phone bills."

Emily laughed. "What if we end up as those horrid Christmas-card friends who only acknowledge each other with a form letter every December?"

"You know that's not going to happen, Em...you hardly ever get your cards in the mail before the end of January."

"I take it back. Maybe I won't miss you."

"You may not have the chance to, anyway. I'm only going for an interview. If they don't offer me the job, you're stuck with me."

"They'd be crazy not to," Emily said loyally.

Joss was about to respond when her door suddenly swung open. She'd pulled it shut, but apparently hadn't latched it completely. Annette Clarion stood in the doorway, her eyes as wide as Joss's.

"Em? Someone just stepped into my office, so I'll talk to you later, okay?"

What had that someone heard? For obvious reasons, Joss hadn't been telling people that a New York firm was recruiting her. Some of the folks around here were still miffed about the way Hugh's predecessor had jumped ship for more sparkling waters.

"Good morning, Annette." she said. Something about "What did you hear?" seemed too paranoid.

"I have these vouchers for you," the other woman said, her expression unreadable. "I was going to knock on your door when it opened."

"N-no problem. Just bring them on in."

After Annette had left the office, Joss pressed a hand to her forehead. Kimmerman hadn't objected in the least to her request of taking a personal day Friday, but she knew his tolerant attitude would take a sharp turn if he found out why she'd asked. She hoped they liked her in New York…she hated the thought of coming home from a failed interview to find herself out of a job.

Despite her impressive credentials, her résumé was beginning to look as spotty as her romantic track record.

WITH THE EXCEPTION of meetings about the Lynwood account, which had been attended by a handful of key employees, Joss had managed to avoid much direct contact with Hugh throughout the week. And that was the way she wanted it, she told herself as she finished packing Thursday night.

Emily thought Joss should try to talk to him, but Emily was looking through the rose-colored glasses of love. In this one instance, Joss was going to show Hugh that she was capable of leaving well enough alone and not trying to build more. He'd probably been right—they would drive each other nuts.

On the other hand, every time she'd sat in one of those meetings, she'd felt as if she was betraying Hugh personally. They were planning for the future of the Lynwood campaign, but it was possible she wouldn't be around for that future. And if Annette *had* overheard something that would come out in office gossip, Joss would rather Hugh got the news straight from her first. They may have their differences, but she trusted him to keep this confidence.

She plopped down on her comforter with a sigh and picked up the phone. It was telling that she still had his home number committed to memory after all the time that had gone by since she'd last used it. She dialed the first couple of digits, but then almost lost her nerve.

This couldn't possibly be harder than going to talk to Vivian, right? *And look how well that turned out.* Right. She could do this. How many times could the same guy make you nervous, anyway? When would she reach the point where she was unaffected by him?

But she couldn't imagine a time when seeing

Hugh wouldn't cause a little tremor in her stomach, a time when just hearing his voice would make her almost smile as she sensed a wisecrack coming, a time when looking into those impossibly blue eyes—

"If you would like to make a call, please hang up and dial again."

Joss jumped, glaring at the phone and the mechanical operator. She punched the buttons quickly this time with a renewed sense of purpose. He'd answer, she'd get this over with and maybe she'd feel a sense of closure. Maybe that was why she couldn't imagine moving on completely.

Or, just a thought, braniac, maybe it's because you're in love with him and you're pretty sure he's the only man you've ever loved. But why quibble over details?

"Hi, this is Hugh—"

"Hey, it's—" She stopped abruptly when she realized she was identifying herself to an answering machine. Hallelujah. His not being there was perfect. She could just leave her message and make her escape.

She dutifully waited for the beep, then started over. "Hey, it's Joss. You probably weren't expecting to hear from me…"

"…SO WISH ME LUCK. And, Hugh, no hard feelings, okay?" Hugh stared at the phone until he heard the soft click of her hanging up. When he'd first turned off the shower, he'd thought he was losing his mind.

Guys being mostly visual creatures, he pictured Joss in his head all the time, but hearing voices was new. And a touch disturbing. After a moment, though, he'd realized he was listening to her on the answering machine. He'd wrapped his towel around his waist and dashed into his bedroom. Yet when he got there, he hadn't picked up the receiver.

All week long, he'd been torturing himself with the hurt expression on her face when he'd told her that he thought they might have made a mistake, that she was too uptight for him. She hadn't betrayed much emotion at the office this week, but just now, in her message, she'd sounded as though she was finally in a good place. Maybe New York, with its pace and wealth of opportunities, would be perfect for her. Why talk to her and mess that up, risk upsetting her again?

Still, as he finished getting ready to go to his brother's, he had to admit he would miss her like crazy. The thought of her office sitting empty down the hall from his was more upsetting than he would've imagined, considering it had only been hers for a few weeks. Then he realized he was being ridiculous—Kimmerman would hire someone to replace her. The office wouldn't stay empty, but the image of someone else in Joss's chair behind Joss's desk was worse than the room going unused.

Maybe she won't get the job in New York.

Right. And maybe summer wouldn't be hot in Texas this year. He was talking about *Joss*. She would dazzle them all in New York with her one hundred and ten percent commitment, the very determination Hugh had mocked.

As he drove to Craig's, his guilt rode shotgun. Dreams were good for people, and if Joss's was to open her own agency, he should have respected that. No way in hell did he want to be part of it, but still...

Her plans had taken him by surprise, but what she didn't know was that his first, unexpressed, reaction had been enthusiasm. It had only lasted for a millisecond, but even the fraction of a moment had been enough to scare him.

He'd immediately thought of names, letterhead, the contacts they could pool between them, and his mental overdrive had reminded him of all the things he'd said he wasn't going to be anymore. There was more to life than frantically chasing success at the expense of actually living and taking the time to be happy. He wanted to take weekends off to enjoy himself, spend dinners with beautiful women discussing something *other* than advertising. Which meant he was probably the wrong man for Joss.

When he reached his older brother's house, Hugh realized that it had been a while since his last visit. For a few months last year, Craig, Hugh and Mitch had had a regular weekly poker game, but that had somehow fallen apart. Both of his brothers had been surprised but agreeable when Hugh suggested playing tonight. Hugh wasn't sure if it was nostalgia, brought on by thinking so much about his family recently, or if he just needed something to help take his mind off Joss—a strategy that really would have worked better if he didn't spend the better part of the next three hours whining about her.

Around ten, Mitch tossed his cards onto the dining-room table. "I fold. Anybody else want another beer from the kitchen?"

"I'll take one," Craig said. "And bring one for Mopey here, too."

Hugh shook his head, somewhat perturbed by the

way the room spun. "More beer will just make me maudlin."

Craig snorted. "You hit maudlin about an hour ago. At this point, I'm just hoping more beer will make you pass out."

Standing in the doorway of the kitchen, Mitch nodded. "Honestly, bro, why don't you just put together a country-music demo and be done with it? That's how depressing you are."

"I couldn't carry a tune with a permit…you know who *can* sing, though?"

"Joss," both his brothers chorused.

Hugh winced at their exasperated tones. Lord, he really was making a fool of himself tonight. "Guess I already told you the karaoke story, huh?"

"No." Craig shook his head. "But with the one track your mind's been on all night, it wasn't a tough deduction. Do you even realize how much money you've lost?"

Hugh blinked. "Lost?" He didn't lose. In fact, now that he thought about it, that might have been the reason their original weekly games had stopped.

Craig pushed back his chair, standing into a full-body stretch. "I think you've paid my cable bill for next month. You should come over every time you have girl trouble."

"I don't normally *have* girl trouble," he muttered. But Joss was like a thorn in his side…a thorn with sexy wit and a hot body to match. "And I don't normally lose."

"Too true," Craig agreed, grabbing the cold bottle of beer Mitch held out his way. "I used to despise you for that."

"For beating you?" Hugh was relieved his older

brother didn't sound angry about it. In fact, Craig seemed to have found a new peace in his life, and Hugh knew he wouldn't spend as much time worrying in the next few months as he had in the ones following the heart attack.

"No, not just for beating me—"

"Although that did always suck," Mitch chimed in.

"But for not understanding what it was like," Craig said. "I would resent the hell out of you for never having to struggle with anything."

Well, he'd certainly struggled with his feelings for Joss…trying to get her to reconsider, only to botch things up once she did. He'd had some legitimate points, but he'd walked out so quickly it was hard to say whether or not they could have overcome them. He was used to things being easier.

Joss was difficult.

And stunning. He loved her wicked, wry humor. He loved the way she cared about others and the fire she put into her job, never just marking time until the proverbial five o'clock whistle. He loved the way she worried about that obnoxious cat of hers. He—*oh, God*—loved Joss.

The fact of the matter was, a relationship with her would require work, on both their parts, but if love wasn't worth any effort, what was?

JOCELYN TAPPED her driver's license against the palm of her hand, waiting for her turn in the security line at DFW. The weather forecast she'd got on-line said that New York was supposed to have snow today, a rare treat for someone from Texas, but she wasn't sure yet how she'd feel about living in an area where—

"J! Jocelyn, wait!"

Her mind blanked. She only knew one person who called her J, particularly in that husky bedroom voice, still recognizable despite the odd note of panic it held today. She turned slowly, trying to process this unexpected scenario.

Hugh, unshaven and looking a bit worse for wear, was barreling toward her. "Wait! Joss, don't go yet."

She raised her hands in a nonchalant shrug. "The line's not even moving, Hugh."

But he didn't slow his approach, and apparently she wasn't the only one who found his behavior strange. Two uniformed members of airport security began to move toward the scruffy agitated man. Eyes wide, Joss hurried out of line, ready to vouch for Hugh.

"It's all right, officers—um, sirs? I just, ah, forgot something, and my friend here was returning it before my flight."

Both men turned skeptical glances toward her, and she knew without being told that she'd have to hand over her shoes for inspection when she went through the metal detector. Hopefully, the pumps would be *all* she had to remove.

The burlier of the two men—which was a lot like saying the richer of the two billionaires—raised his eyebrows. "If he doesn't have a boarding pass, I'll need the two of you to step aside and resume your place in line only when you're ready to go on to the terminal."

Hugh nodded. "Got it. Absolutely. Thank you." Then he turned his bloodshot eyes to Joss. "I'm so glad I caught you in time."

"What is wrong with you? You look like you've been out drinking all night."

He sat down in a chair against the wall. "That's what happens when you stay out drinking all night, I guess. Mitch and I had this great plan that I'd be here first thing in the morning, ahead of you. But we all kind of crashed around three in the morning, so I overslept. Craig just dropped me off a few minutes ago."

"Why?" She'd say this for him, he'd broken up the monotony of the airport routine. But she'd yet to identify a reason for his bizarre behavior.

"Joss, I don't want you to go to New York."

Warmth stole through her body; she felt as if she must be glowing. "Really? That's... You do know I'm coming back this weekend, right? We could have talked then."

Hugh grabbed her hand, tugging her down into the row of chairs beside him. "I couldn't wait anymore. We should have talked a year ago. When I hurt you the first time. If I hadn't had my head so far up my ass, I would've apologized."

"You mean about the salon account?" Maybe *she'd* overslept, too, and was dreaming all this.

"Sort of. You were legitimately tapped out of ideas, and I'm not sorry I had one that got the company the contract. But I could've handled it better, been more understanding. Something. I never should have let you go, but I was so wrapped up in my career then, in winning and looking forward to the next step on the ladder."

She thought about everything he'd said to her in the last month and sighed. "You mean all the stuff I'm wrapped up in now?"

"No." He squeezed her hand, then laced his fingers through hers. She was in danger of missing her plane if she stayed here much longer, but she didn't care. "You're driven, but that's never stopped you from being concerned about others. You made a point of looking after your Visions co-workers when they came to Kimmerman. You want good things for your friends. Maybe you're a pain in the—"

She raised an eyebrow.

"Wait, that might not have the romantic note I was going for. What I'm trying to say is, whatever your flaws—not that you have many—your heart's in the right place. And your heart is what's most important to me. I love you, Joss."

Tears spilled over her cheeks, so sudden she didn't even have a chance to try to hold them at bay. "You mean that?"

"No, I routinely burst into airports at 6 a.m. looking like death on toast."

She sniffed. "And smelling a little like it, too. But I love you, anyway."

He crushed her to him in a hug that made her heart swell. "I know I'm not perfect, J. I'm never gonna be. But if you can live with that, then I am capable of exerting the effort a successful relationship takes."

"I'll let you in on a secret," she whispered. "I like you the way you are, imperfections and all."

"If you really want to move to New York—"

She shook her head. "My only family's here, and a house I really love and my best friend. I just agreed to do this interview because I felt like something was missing."

"But?"

"I've figured out what it was. Thank you." She grinned. "Why don't I call Slossinger, let him know I won't be able to make it? Then we can go somewhere more private, and I can practice 'having fun.'"

He stood, pulling her up with him and wrapping her in his arms. "There's just one thing I have to do first."

Brushing his knuckles over her cheek, he leaned down to kiss her softly. He tasted like cinnamon gum and second chances, and Joss was so happy she almost laughed, just because it was hard to contain what she felt. Kissing him back was a better option, though. She opened her mouth beneath his and for that one moment, everything in her life *was* perfect.

Joss was in heaven. Who knew it would look so much like an airport?